"It's ridicu
you go t

The bitterness in his tone made
Justine wince. "Like mother, like
daughter."

Justine steadied herself, trying to
hide the hurt, amazed that the lovely
warm feeling had dissolved so swiftly.
"If you think you can manhandle me
whenever it takes your fancy, think
again!" she said vehemently.

His hands again moved over her,
molding her against him. When she
moaned, his smile was triumphant. "I
don't think you'll have the strength to
resist, just as my father couldn't resist
your mother."

"Forewarned is forearmed," she tossed
out. "I shall make sure you don't come
within touching distance ever again."

A muscle worked spasmodically in his
jaw. "Do you think you'll be able to
stop me?"

MARGARET MAYO began writing quite by chance when the engineering company she worked for wasn't very busy, and she found herself with time on her hands. Today, with more than thirty romance novels to her credit, she admits that writing governs her life to a large extent. When she and her husband holiday—Cornwall is their favorite spot—Margaret always has a notebook and camera on hand and is constantly looking for fresh ideas. She lives in the countryside near Stafford, England.

Books by Margaret Mayo

HARLEQUIN ROMANCE

MARGARET MAYO

passionate vengeance

Harlequin Books

TORONTO • NEW YORK • LONDON
AMSTERDAM • PARIS • SYDNEY • HAMBURG
STOCKHOLM • ATHENS • TOKYO • MILAN

Harlequin Presents first edition March 1987
ISBN 0-373-10963-6

Original hardcover edition published in 1986
by Mills & Boon Limited

CHAPTER ONE

A FROWN creased Justine's brow, and her blue eyes narrowed disbelievingly. 'You're dismissing me? Without even giving me a chance to defend myself? You can't do that.'

'I can, and I am.' Mr Smart inclined his head, his smooth grey hair shiny, his narrow foxy face serious. 'In any case, your work hasn't been up to standard recently. That's a good enough excuse.'

'My mother died,' said Justine quietly, 'and I——'

'I'm well aware of that,' cut in Mr Smart, none too gently, 'but life has to go on.'

Justine could also have told him that after the tragic car accident, she'd discovered that the man she had always called father was not her real father at all. The news was a tremendous shock and had certainly affected her emotions for quite a while afterwards. Was it any wonder her work had suffered?

Mr Smart stood up now, the discussion over so far as he was concerned. 'I must admit I never expected it of you, Miss Jamieson. Was your salary so insufficient that you had to sell your ideas to one of our competitors? Or have you been living beyond your means? I know what you young people are like.'

Justine rose also, tossing her head and glaring at the Managing Director. Her short black hair framed her pretty face, which at that moment had two spots of high colour burning in the cheeks. She had never felt so outraged in her life. 'I didn't do it, Mr Smart. If you'd just tell me who made this false accusation, I——'

'There's no point.' He handed her an envelope. 'I

had my information from a very reliable source, and I see no reason to question it. Naturally you'll deny everything, that's human nature. Your salary is here, up to date. Good day, Miss Jamieson.'

It was also human nature to fight for one's honour, but Justine knew it would be a losing battle. He had not let her say one word in her own defence. She might as well leave with her head held high.

All eyes were on Justine as she crammed her few personal possessions into her bag; not many, the favourite knife she had used throughout college, her folder of designs which had helped her get the job in the first place, odds and ends of makeup—the sort of things that accumulated over the years.

She walked out of the building without speaking; too emotional, too afraid she might burst into tears. She did not want anyone to see her break down.

But by the time she reached her flat, anger had set in, so deep that it frightened her. Lies had been told. Why would she want to sell her designs elsewhere? She was happy at Dean & Grace, and had no reason to harm their reputation. The shoes they made were exclusive and expensive, and she was rightly proud to work for them.

She had heard of innocent people being incriminated, but had never imagined she would be the victim of such a cruel lie. Someone must hate her very much, enough to want her out of the company. But who? So far as she was aware, she had no enemies.

It was a distressing situation and Justine was determined to do something about it, but several telephone calls later was no wiser. All her colleagues within the company were as shocked as she by her instant dismissal, and all promised to find out what they could.

'They can't do this to you,' said Penny, her closest friend.

'They already have,' returned Justine bitterly.

'You could take them to court for unfair dismissal.'

'Mr Smart is very sure of himself,' Justine confirmed. 'He'll find proof if he needs it. I can't fight a company like Dean & Grace.'

Her first priority was finding another job. It would not be easy. Vacancies for shoe designers were few and far between, and she had been lucky with Dean & Grace. Penny had told her that one of the designers was leaving to have a baby, and Justine had applied before the job was advertised.

That had been three years ago. She had just obtained her degree after a three-year course, and Dean's had felt that a young, fresh approach might be beneficial.

Justine had proved them right, soon becoming a very valuable member of the design team. Now, like a bolt from the blue, she had been cruelly and coldly dismissed—without even being given a chance to stick up for herself.

She spent a restless, sleepless night, rising the next morning with a determination not to let it get her down.

Phoning several shoe manufacturers within a tube ride of her smart London flat secured her two interviews, and she felt hopeful in both cases. It was a disappointment, therefore, to be informed a few days later that her applications had been unsuccessful.

She tried further afield, but the results were always the same. The firms seemed interested at the time of the interview, but eventually wrote to say that after due consideration they felt she was not suitable.

It became evident that word had got around about her dismissal and she was now unemployable. Someone had really got a knife in her back. She wished she knew who. None of her friends at Dean & Grace had been able to find out anything. Whoever was

instrumental in her dismissal made sure it was kept a
closely guarded secret.

Days turned into weeks and Justine grew desperate.
She could not keep up the payments on her car and
was forced to sell it, even though this limited the area
where she could seek work. Dean & Grace had been
convenient in that respect, their offices situated not
half a mile from where she lived. It was why she had
chosen the flat in the first place. Then she fell behind
with her rent and faced eviction.

Soon the only choice left open to her was to ask
Gerald Jamieson whether she could make her home
with him once again. This was something she was
reluctant to do, because they had never got on, but not
until he told her he wasn't her natural father had she
understood the reason why.

Already grief-stricken by her mother's death,
Justine had been shattered by the news. It also made
many things clear. Her younger brother he adored,
because Stewart was his own flesh and blood.
Apparently Delphine had been pregnant with Justine
when Gerald met and married her, and for reasons he
didn't divulge he had agreed to bring the child up as
his own. He had never loved Justine, though, and after
his disclosure she moved out.

Living on her own had proved more difficult than
she expected. Dean & Grace were not exactly
renowned for paying high salaries, but by stringent
budgeting she had somehow got through. Now she
was penniless and as good as homeless. Her landlord
had given her seven days to find somewhere else.

On the very last day, when Gerald seemed her only
hope, she was contacted by Warrender's. They were
one of the largest shoe manufacturers in the country—
in the world, in fact—and Justine had already tried
them, only to be told there were no vacancies.

Now the letter stated that one had suddenly arisen

and invited her, if she was still interested, to telephone
Mr Warrender's secretary to arrange a mutually
convenient interview. Justine was overjoyed and rang
immediately. The meeting was arranged that same
morning for eleven.

She dressed with care in a cream knitted dress which
suited her ivory complexion and heavy black hair. She
applied faint blue eyeshadow, a touch of mascara and a
rose-pink lipstick, then brushed her hair until it shone
like a raven's wing.

A quarter of an hour before the appointed time, she
arrived at Warrender's. Their offices were in an
impressive tower block with a black marble frontage,
the name 'Warrender's Shoes' embossed in gold
lettering on the glass doors.

Justine felt very nervous. There had been so many
disappointments, but this time she was determined
that nothing would go wrong.

She would be perfectly open with Mr Warrender,
tell him exactly why she had lost her previous job and
assure him that there was not a grain of truth in the
accusation.

This was her last chance. If she failed she'd be
eating humble pie in front of Gerald Jamieson—and
she could well imagine his reception. She would be
tolerated, but that was all. It would not be a happy
life.

Finally the call came for her to enter Mr
Warrender's office. She had no idea what to expect;
someone a little like Smarty Fox, she supposed,
unconsciously using Mr Smart's nickname. In his
fifties or sixties, sharp, intent only on getting the best
out of his staff, not too particular whose feelings he
trod on in the process.

It was a big shock, therefore, to be confronted by a
ferociously handsome man in his mid to late thirties,
nothing at all like her preconception of the owner of

world-famous Warrender's Shoes, Mitchell Warrender.

His dark eyes were razor-sharp, his hair as coal-black as her own, thick and straight, swept to one side. His nose was straight, the jaw square, his lower lip full and sensual.

There was a hint of arrogance in the angle of his head. He looked merciless. Those eyes missed nothing. Deep-set, bridged by thick black brows, piercing in their intensity.

For almost a minute there was silence as he studied her. It seemed an eternity. Justine felt as if she were being dissected, piece by piece, each tiny part of her examined and assessed.

She felt uneasy. Why was he doing this? Was it his intention to unnerve her? Was he trying to test what she was made of?

Lifting her chin she suffered his examination, hiding the conflicting emotions raging inside her—outrage, anger, embarrassment, and more. But she wanted the job, didn't she? She must put up with his insolence.

Finally he spoke. 'Well, Miss Jamieson, you're exactly what I expected.' His deep voice seemed to send tiny shock waves down Justine's spine.

She looked at him, her fine brows raised questioningly. He was certainly different from what she had expected, but it was news that he had already formed an opinion about her.

'Should I be flattered?' The words were out before she could stop them.

'I doubt it.'

Justine flinched at the sharpness of his tone. 'I'm sorry. I spoke without thinking.'

'Is that a habit of yours?'

Again the words were fired like bullets from a gun. His eyes never once left her face as he appraised her and her answer.

'Not usually.' There was something about this man that made her react in a totally alien manner.

'That's good. I don't take kindly to my employees shooting their mouths off.'

'I am not your employee yet,' said Justine defensively.

'But you are interested in the job?'

She shrugged. 'You know I am.' But would she be happy? For some unknown reason she had taken an instant dislike to Mr Warrender—and he to her, though why was anyone's guess. Did he already know the reason she had left Dean & Grace? Was he holding it against her? If so, why ask her here today? Had he a sadistic streak? Did he want to humiliate her some more? His attitude made no sense at all.

He sat down suddenly at his desk, gesturing her to take the seat in front of him. She did so willingly, her legs feeling as though they could support her weight no longer.

He was obviously a sexually aggressive man who dressed to leave women in no doubt of his physical attraction. The fine material of his trousers clung slavishly to each and every muscle in his thighs, emphasising the length of his legs. His ice-blue shirt was unbuttoned at the neck, sleeves rolled back to expose sinewy arms covered by fine dark hair. It was impossible not to feel a sensual awareness of him.

'Tell me, Miss Jamieson, why are you looking for a job? Are you not happy in your present employment?'

His innocent expression did not fool her for one moment. He knew she was out of work and he was testing her. He wanted to see whether she would tell the truth.

She looked down at her hands, heart pounding. 'I was dismissed.'

'Oh?'

'For something I did not do.' She looked up at him challengingly now.

'And you let them get rid of you? Why didn't you defend yourself?' His eyes narrowed until they were no more than slits. He reminded her of a tiger—and no doubt he was just as dangerous!

Justine did her best to hold his gaze. 'I was given no chance.'

His brows rose and his eyes widened. 'You expect me to believe that? There are laws to protect people against unfair dismissal.'

'Mr Smart seemed to think he had some pretty solid evidence. He virtually dared me to try it.'

'Mr Smart—of Dean & Grace? Was that where you worked?'

'I think you already know that, Mr Warrender.'

For several long seconds they eyed each other—and then he smiled, a cold soulless smile that never made it to his eyes. 'You're right. You're more astute than I thought, though it's not entirely unexpected under the circumstances.'

What did he mean by that cryptic remark? Justine frowned and stared at him but he gave no explanation, merely continuing, 'So what makes you think I might give you employment?'

Justine shrugged. 'I have no reason to think you will, except that I suspect you already knew my circumstances when you sent for me.'

'You're a good designer, I'm told. And I felt that you should be given a fair chance, provided you told me the truth about yourself.'

'So I've got the job?' Justine could not prevent a smile from spreading across her face. She jumped up from her seat. 'Oh, Mr Warrender, you don't know how happy that makes me!' It meant she wouldn't have to leave her flat; that she wouldn't have to beg the hateful Gerald Jamieson to take her back. It was more than she had dared hope.

There was no answering smile on the dark man's face, no evidence of pleasure. 'Wait until you hear what's involved before you sing for joy.'

Justine's euphoria did not fade. Whatever it was, it had to be better than being unemployed. 'I don't care,' she exulted.

His lips curled in a downward sneer. 'You're that desperate?'

She could not believe he did not guess. He was taunting her. For reasons known only to himself, he wanted to humiliate her.

'I'm on the verge of being thrown out of my flat,' she said quietly, 'for not paying the rent. That's how desperate I am.'

Was that a fleeting smile she saw crossing his face—gone so swiftly she must have imagined it?

'So if I take you on, I'm an angel in disguise?'

There was no mistaking the sardonic humour now, but anything less like an angel was difficult to imagine. With his chiselled, angular features he was more like a devil.

'I don't think I'd exactly say that,' she feinted, 'but it would help.'

'You do realise you'd be a very junior designer in a very experienced team? And that consequently the salary won't be all that high?'

It had to be better than Dean & Grace paid. Warrender's was a household name. 'Warrender's Walk the World' was their proud motto. Everyone had heard of Warrender's. Dean & Grace were one of the smaller companies in the shoe-manufacturing business.

But when he actually mentioned the sum he intended paying her, Justine gasped. It was a pittance; no one could live on such a meagre wage.

'Are you serious?' she breathed.

Solemnly, Mitchell Warrender nodded. 'Take it or leave it, the choice is yours. So far as I'm concerned, I'm doing you a favour. No one else will employ you, isn't that right?'

Glumly, Justine nodded. But how would she manage unless her landlord reduced the rent? It was highly improbable, but she would have to ask.

'And the hours are eight till six, five days a week— Saturdays as well if the work demands it.'

Justine could not believe she was hearing him correctly. What was he, a slave-driver? No one worked such long hours, unless they were paid overtime. But it *was* a job and she needed one desperately. Even this was better than living with Gerald. She made no argument.

'I'll take it,' she said faintly.

He pushed himself briskly to his feet. 'You're sure?' She nodded.

He came round the desk and held out his hand. Justine ignored it. She could not shake on a deal that was a penance. Warrender was evil. He was taking advantage of her situation, getting himself a good designer without having to pay the going rate.

But maybe if she did her job well, he would relent and increase her salary in proportion to the hours she worked? She could understand his hesitation—after all, it was her word against Smarty Fox's. He probably knew the man and preferred to trust him rather than herself.

Heavens, why was she defending him? He was doing her no favours. He was on to a good thing and well he knew it. He was either in on the tale that she had sold to competitors, and knew there was no truth behind it, or he intended having her under surveillance twenty-four hours a day to make sure she did not repeat the foul deed.

Whichever way his thoughts ran, she was at his

mercy. If she wanted the job, she had no choice but to agree to his terms.

'I'll see you in the morning, then,' he said with one of his mirthless smiles.

Justine inclined her head. Her pleasure at finding a job had faded. His less than generous offer cancelled out her joy.

Nevertheless, she put on a brave face when she approached her landlord a short time later. But he was interested only in making money. Justine's plight meant nothing to him. 'If you can't pay the rent, you're out,' he snarled.

'Okay, I'll pay it,' sighed Justine, wondering why she had ever thought she could appeal to his better nature. It would mean having next to nothing left for food, but she would manage, somehow.

She spent a restless night, the hateful Mr Warrender never out of her thoughts. Other women might find him attractive, but she didn't. Why, then, did his face keep floating before her mind's eye? What was it about him that could not be ignored?

His aggression? His obvious dislike of her? The fact that he had offered her a job despite his personal feelings? There was something not quite right about the situation, but she could not figure out what it was.

Sleep finally overtook her, though dreams disturbed it, and she woke feeling dazed and groggy. But a hot cup of tea put her right, and when she finally set out there was a spring in her step.

She made up her mind to enjoy the job no matter what. She didn't object to hard work—it was being taken advantage of that annoyed her. When Mr Warrender saw what a good worker she was he would have a change of heart and revise her salary. It would be all right, she knew it would.

So she arrived in optimistic mood. The girl in

reception told her where to go, and she entered the lift
and pressed the button for the third floor.

She stepped out on to a carpeted corridor, and the
first person she saw was Mr Warrender. She had not
expected him to be here so early, nor to meet her. It
was almost as though he was waiting. A gleam
lightened his eyes. 'This way, Miss Jamieson. I'm glad
to see you're on time.'

Justine bit back a hasty retort and smiled instead.
She must not jeopardise the job at this stage. 'I always
try to be punctual,' she said lightly.

As he led the way along the corridor to the Design
Department, Justine felt once again a physical
awareness of him. Whether she liked the man or not,
there was no disputing his male magnetism.

She had never experienced such an immediate
response, at least not so early in a relationship. No
boyfriend had ever triggered off this very positive
reaction. It was puzzling, to say the least.

'Mr Hunt is my chief designer,' Warrender threw
over his shoulder as he strode ahead. 'He knows all
about you.'

Meaning he had been put in the picture regarding
her past record, and no doubt instructed to keep an
eagle eye on her.

Justine compressed her lips, hurrying to keep up
with her employer's long stride. She would be very
much on probation here, that was clear, and in all
fairness she could not blame him. How she wished she
knew who it was who had done this to her!

He pushed open a door, holding it for Justine to
enter, eyeing her darkly as she moved past him. Of
its own volition, Justine's heartbeat stepped up and
she felt cross with herself for responding in this
manner.

There was a mutual feeling of distrust between
them, so why couldn't she control these strange urges?

With her head held high, she caught the eye of a man on the other side of the room.

Desmond Hunt was tall and gentle-looking, with fair hair going grey, soft blue eyes and a welcoming smile. Justine felt an overwhelming relief to see at least one friendly face.

Mitchell Warrender gave the other man a curt nod. 'This is Miss Jamieson, the new designer I told you about. I'll leave her to you.' With that, he turned and disappeared.

For a second it felt as though something was missing, so strong was his impact on Justine; then she took the hand Desmond Hunt offered and Mitchell Warrender was forgotten.

'Welcome to the team, Justine. You don't mind if I call you that? We don't hold with formalities.'

'Please do,' she smiled, his manner putting her instantly at ease.

'I believe you used to design for Dean & Grace? The work here is not quite so upmarket. We cater for the masses—though not at the expense of style and quality, I hasten to add.'

'Mr Warrender has told you why I left?' ventured Justine, still feeling a need to keep everything in the open.

He nodded solemnly. 'But it's no business of mine. Mr Warrender must trust you, otherwise he wouldn't have taken you on.'

'I didn't do it,' said Justine simply. 'And I can't tell you how grateful I am to Mr Warrender. I'd almost given up hope of finding another job.'

Desmond Hunt smiled. 'Well, at least you have one now, and I'm sure you'll do well.'

Justine wished she felt as confident. There was something about Mitchell Warrender's attitude that bothered her. He had offered her work, yet hadn't seemed to happy about it. But, determinedly, she pushed these thoughts to the back of her mind, and the rest of the day passed quickly and happily.

There were eight members of the team, and they were all friendly and helpful, so that by the end of her first week's employment Justine felt as though she had been there for a month.

Mitchell Warrender left for the States without her seeing him again, and all was peaceful—except for her landlord. He was like a man possessed, chasing her for the rent arrears each time he caught sight of her. He seemed to think that because she now had a job she could pay up, refusing to accept that she did not earn enough.

There was nothing for it but to find somewhere cheaper. She had been brought up in a fine house with a high standard of living and appreciated the nice things in life—but even lowering her standards would be preferable to living again with Gerald Jamieson at Holt House.

When Mr Warrender returned, he sent for her. Glancing shrewdly at her shadowed eyes and pallid complexion, 'You're not enjoying the job?' he queried.

'The job's fine,' she said quietly. His tan had deepened, complemented by the white shirt, open necked as usual, sleeves rolled back. She caught a hint of muscled chest, a scattering of dark hairs, and when her eyes returned to his face he was watching her.

Faint colour tinged her cheeks and she hoped he did not think she was interested in him. It was just that he was different from anyone else. There was an indefinable something that attracted her whether she liked it or not.

'You don't look well. You've lost weight.' It was his turn to survey her—and he took his time about it, not missing one inch of her anatomy—her long legs and slender hips, her tiny waist and delicately rounded breasts.

It irritated her to be scrutinised like this and she frowned, tossing her head, her short, thick hair bouncing, blue eyes flashing. 'I'm sure my health can be of no concern to you, Mr Warrender.'

'It could cause your work to suffer.' There was a hint of steel in his dark eyes, a suggestion that she would be out before she had time to draw breath if such a thing should happen.

'It won't,' she said abruptly, 'I'll make sure of that.'

'Are you not sleeping well? Does the work worry you?'

Justine eyed him guardedly. Why all these questions? Of what particular concern could her welfare be to him? 'I'm enjoying it very much, Mr Warrender, and Mr Hunt seems satisfied. My private life is my own affair. I have no wish to discuss it with you.'

His lips tightened at her abrupt manner. 'The right is yours,' he agreed coolly, 'but you look as though a square meal won't do you any harm. I'll pick you up at seven-thirty.'

Justine's chin jerked upward. Now what was he up to? 'Thank you for the offer, but I have something planned for tonight.'

'Then cancel it,' he barked.

'Why?' A frown creased her brow, and her blue eyes reflected her puzzlement. 'Why do you want to take me out?'

His gaze held hers for several long seconds. 'I have my reasons.'

But he was not prepared to discuss them with her. The thought of a good meal was tempting, though. She had eaten hardly enough to keep her alive this last week, handing most of her salary over to her landlord.

'Do I have a choice?' she enquired faintly.

'No.' That one word was final.

Justine shrugged. 'In that case, I accept.' But she did not expect to enjoy the evening. There was something coldly calculating behind Mitchell Warrender's eyes, something she could not fathom, something that frightened her.

'Good.' His lips curved briefly. 'You may go now. I shall look forward to tonight.'

Like hell he would, thought Justine. Mitchell Warrender needed watching closely. He would not issue the invitation for nothing. Perhaps he wanted to find out more about her dismissal from Dean & Grace? Perhaps he thought good food and wine would loosen her tongue? If that was so he was in for a shock, because she could tell him no more than he already knew.

As she showered and dressed, Justine could not help wondering what the evening held in store. It was a long time since she had been out with anyone like Mitchell Warrender. After leaving Holt House, she had mixed with an entirely different set of people. None of them was rich, all were struggling to make ends meet, and when she had gone out on a date she had more often than not paid her share.

Tonight would be different. Under other circumstances she would have enjoyed the prospect—but with Mitchell Warrender? That was a moot question.

At seven-thirty on the dot, he arrived. Justine let him in and he eyed her unreservedly. The blue of her dress matched her eyes, made them dance with a brilliance that had been missing of late.

The dress was of a fine, soft material with a pretty scalloped neckline and hem. It was feminine and romantic and she wondered whether it was right for the occasion. It was one of her mother's—she and Delphine had often swapped clothes—and after her death Justine had added most of them to her own wardrobe.

As she had known would happen, Justine felt an immediate warmth spread in the pit of her stomach, tiny spirals of excitement slowly rising. He was indisputably virile—and for the next hour or so would be her sole companion.

It was a foolish excitement, because the evening could be disastrous. He had not invited her out because he was attracted to her—far from it. There was an underlying reason—and very soon she would find out what it was.

He still studied her, nodding slowly to himself, and she wondered what he was thinking.

'Will I do?' she asked, when she could stand his scrutiny no longer.

He smiled, a sardonic twisted smile, his eyes lit by a strange light. 'You look exactly as I imagined.'

'What do you mean?' she frowned. 'You speak as though it's the first time you've seen me.'

'The first time I've seen you dressed up. I knew you'd wear something designed to captivate.'

A cold shiver ran down Justine's spine. 'That was not my intention at all. This simply happens to be a favourite dress.'

'And one in which you break many hearts?'

His dry tones were not lost on her. 'That is not my habit, Mr Warrender.'

'You're twenty-four and unmarried?'

She eyed him with hostility. 'I trust you're not suggesting what I think? If it's your intention to insult me, then don't bother taking me out.'

'You're very beautiful when you're angry—even more like——' He broke off suddenly, as though he'd said more than he intended. 'Come along, it's time we went.'

Justine followed him, pondering over his half-formed sentence. Whom was she like? Someone he knew? Was that the reason for his interest? Did she remind him of a person who had hurt him? That would explain why he did not seem to like her, but not his motive for asking her out.

Mitchell Warrender's car was long, expensive and powerful—like himself, and Justine sank back in her seat as it surged forward.

His distinctive woody aftershave teased her nostrils and she guessed would remind her for ever of him. It was all she could do to keep her eyes on the road ahead.

There was something magnetically attractive about this man, and despite her good intentions Justine found herself glancing curiously across at him. In profile, his face looked different. Still arrogant, but his features seemed softer. The chiselled cheekbones were not so clearly visible, nor was the hardness of his eyes so acute. He looked kinder, more human, and almost approachable.

'Whom do I remind you of?' she asked, fingers mentally crossed for a favourable reply.

There was a moment's silence before he answered, and in that short space Justine felt the full impact of his dislike. The impression was so strong that she felt cold all over and wished she had never spoken.

'I don't think now is the time or place to tell you.' A muscle jerked in his jaw, and his whole body tensed with an emotion she could not understand. 'But I will, make no mistake about that. *And you'll wish you'd never met me.*'

CHAPTER TWO

AT that moment Justine knew the whole evening was doomed, and wished with all her heart she'd had the courage to refuse to come out with Mitchell Warrender. Exactly whom did she remind him of? It was a tormenting question which he did not intend answering in a hurry—and until he did, she was at his mercy.

It was clear now why he had offered her this job; not because he needed another designer but simply to get his hands on her. What wasn't clear, was why? Why take it out on her? A chill stole over Justine, but she smiled, trying not to let her companion see how much he disturbed her. 'You sound very sinister. I can't imagine, though, that you're serious.'

He glanced at her, and she would have had to be blind not to see the raw hatred in his eyes. It was gone in a second, replaced by a smile that held no trace of sincerity.

Justine frowned, feeling the skin tighten across her face and scalp. She was cold, deathly cold. He had answered her question without speaking. He had never been more sincere in his life.

'I prefer not to discuss the matter at this moment.'

Justine swallowed. 'I think I'd like to go home.'

His head jerked. 'You're not hungry?'

'Not any more.'

Dark eyes widened. 'But I am. And I'm sure your loss of appetite is only temporary. I didn't intend to disturb you.'

Justine glanced at him sharply. 'You knew very well what you were doing.'

'There are occasions when a man cannot help himself. Please forget I ever said anything.'

Forget! How did he imagine she would do that? He had threatened her, no less—and she was supposed to forget it? 'I'm sorry,' she said, voice tight. 'But that's impossible. However, it would be childish of me to ruin your evening.'

'I'm glad you've come to your senses.' He gave her what looked like a genuine smile, though Justine was now suspicious of all he did or said. When he had first offered her the job she had looked upon him as her saviour. Now she was not so sure.

They remained silent for the rest of the short journey, Justine speculating on the outcome of her association with Mitchell Warrender, which she feared might end in disaster. Mitchell himself, totally undisturbed, was actually humming a jolly tune, as though the whole thing amused him.

By the time they reached the restaurant, Justine was seething, and when he attempted to take her arm she snatched it away.

His reaction was a raised eyebrow, nothing more, though she could guess at the thoughts going through his mind.

The restaurant was French and intimate and she let him do the ordering. Her pre-dinner Martini went straight to her head, as she had eaten nothing all day except a slice of toast. But once she had some food inside her she felt better, actually enjoying the excellent meal and matching Mitchell glass for glass where the wine was concerned.

They discussed the shoe trade in general, Mitchell complimenting her on her refreshingly different ideas—much to Justine's surprise. She wondered whether he wasn't trying to soften the blow when it came?

There was no mention of her dismissal from Dean &

Grace, and she guessed that this was the last thing on his mind now. He had merely used her unemployment as a lever to get her under his control.

It was a very volatile situation and one which she had never envisaged when Mitchell Warrender first sent for her. At the moment he was politeness itself, but how long would it last? He had warned her that one day she would wish she had never met him.

'Brandy?'

'Please.' They reached the coffee stage without one further cross word. He seemed to be doing his best to correct the earlier sinister impression he had made.

Justine felt relaxed. Mitchell was a perfect companion when he set himself out to entertain, and the combination of excellent food, potent wine, and his own particular brand of charm, drugged her senses until she wondered whether her earlier suspicions had been quite imaginary.

He took her home, and when she fumbled in the dark with her key he opened the door for her, following her inside. Justine was in far too mellow a mood to stop him. 'Would you like a coffee?' she asked, 'or perhaps a hot chocolate?' smiling even as she voiced the question. Mitchell Warrender was not a hot chocolate man.

But he surprised her by nodding. 'Hot chocolate's perfect,' and sitting in her most comfortable chair.

As she filled the kettle, Justine could not help reflecting that this evening had been full of surprises—and most surprising of all was her own attitude. It would be fatal to encourage this man after the threat he had issued, and yet she did not seem able to help herself.

When she rejoined him, he was almost asleep. His eyes were closed, black lashes fanning out beneath them, harsh features relaxed. He appeared younger, suddenly vulnerable, and she smiled.

He opened his eyes, looked at her, and sprang up to take the tray with the two steaming cups, positioning it on a low table in front of the settee so that Justine had no choice but to sit at his side.

'May I say what a pleasant room this is? In fact, what a delightful flat. You have excellent taste. Your parents obviously brought you up to appreciate the finer things in life.'

'I suppose they did,' said Justine shortly, not wanting to discuss her mother, or Gerald, with this man.

'Do I detect a note of resentment?' He was quick to pick up the change in her tone. 'Are things not as they should be between you? Is that why you left home?'

Justine picked up her cup. 'I left because my mother died, and I—wanted independence.'

'I'm sorry,' he said quietly. 'But it must have been hard on your father—losing you as well. Didn't you think about that?'

'He didn't care about me,' she said, chin suddenly jutting, her eyes brilliant. 'He never loved me. He was glad to see me go.'

Mitchell took a sip of his drink also, watching her closely over the rim of his cup. 'Were you an only child?'

'I have a brother.'

'And he is still at home?'

She nodded.

'Do you go and see him?'

'No. We meet outside the house. Why are you asking all these questions?'

'Do you object?'

'No.' And, oddly, that was the truth.

'Are you like your mother?'

Justine frowned. His voice was different, not so casual. 'People say I am.'

'Is that her photograph?'

She glanced at the silver-framed picture on the television. 'Yes. It was taken on her fortieth birthday.' She fetched the portrait and handed it to him. 'I hope I look as good when I'm forty. People used to think we were sisters.' In fact, they hadn't been as close as sisters, not even as close as some mothers and daughters. But Justine had loved her mother all the same, and missed her very much.

There was a stillness about him as he studied the likeness. Justine wondered what he was thinking.

'Yes,' he said at length, a new harshness to his voice. 'This could actually be you. It's amazing.'

Justine had grown used to people remarking on their similarity, but Mitchell seemed more struck by it than was usual. There was something else, too, which she could not quite fathom. He was angry for some reason.

Suddenly, he flung the picture to one side. 'I've seen enough.'

Justine uttered a protest at his careless mishandling of her treasured photo. 'Don't do that. You might have broken it.'

She reached across him to retrieve the frame and was caught by surprise when he pulled her roughly into his arms. 'Mr Warrender! What are you——?' Her protest was cut short. As his mouth captured hers, Justine knew she was lost.

From the beginning she had felt and fought against his powerful magnetism, helped by their mutual hostility. But now, sated with good food and wine, her resistance was so low as to be virtually non-existent.

Her mouth opened beneath the pressure of his, his probing tongue sending fresh shivers of anticipation through her. Unable to control herself, she strained against him, and the next moment found herself lying on the couch.

The blue dress was pulled from her shoulders,

exposing her delicately rounded breasts. She watched his face avidly, saw the glitter of desire as he traced their contours, his thumbs urging her nipples into hard throbbing peaks. His mouth quickly followed, teeth nibbling, hurting—but not enough to make her call a halt.

Then once again he captured her mouth, and Justine held him down on top of her, feeling the ripple of muscle beneath her fingertips, aware of his arousal, wondering briefly why she was letting him do this, but not worrying too much about it.

It all seemed so right and natural. It had happened without either of them expecting it. If the truth were known, he was as surprised as she.

Then, without warning, he got to his feet. Justine felt as though part of her had been torn away, and looked at him, wide-eyed. The transformation in him was alarming. His eyes were glacial, his whole face an ugly mask. Even his breathing was ragged.

'What have I done?' she ventured. Judging by his expression it was something awful.

'Reacted as I expected.' He spoke savagely, fingers curled into tight fists, rocking on the balls of his feet. His whole stance was that of a prize-fighter, and Justine wondered whether he intended making her his punchball.

She moved quickly, springing to her feet, tugging her dress back into position and facing him, eyes bright, lips parted. 'Is that abnormal? Do girls usually fight off your advances? Was I too easy? If that's the case, I apologise. It's not my normal practice to fall into the arms of a man at the first sign of an advance.'

'But you found me irresistible?' The sarcasm was scarcely veiled.

'You're physically attractive, as you must know.' Even as she challenged him, an unwitting surge of desire tightened her stomach muscles and she looked away. This was madness.

'And you react like this to any man who is reasonably presentable?'

Justine's head shot round. 'No, I don't. What are you suggesting?' Her lips were tight now, her face flushed with anger.

His lips curled into a sneer. 'I think the answer is obvious. Thank you for confirming my suspicions. It's been a most profitable evening. Good night.' In a couple of strides, he reached the door.

'Wait—you can't——'

But he had gone.

Justine turned angrily back into the room. Damn the man! What game was he playing? What had she confirmed? Her head spun. It was an insane situation. She was totally confused.

Whatever conclusion he had drawn, it all seemed to point back to his obsession that she was like some other girl—someone who had clearly hurt him very much—and he was going to make her, Justine, pay for it!

He was out of his mind. He could not do this. She would not let him. But how could she put a stop to it? Quitting her job was one solution, but she was loath to take it. She would definitely not find another. The only reason she had this one was because of her similarity to the unknown girl who had played such a devastating part in Mitchell Warrender's life.

It was a vicious circle, with her in the middle. Working at Warrender's meant the difference between her living her own independent life or going back to the hateful Gerald Jamieson. The man she had once called father would certainly make her life a misery. Life in his house could be even worse than putting up with this abuse.

Justine washed the cups, took a shower, and went to bed but sleep would not come. The events of the

evening revolved in her head, becoming mixed and
distorted, until finally she got up.

Two cups of tea and a half hour later she finally
managed to drop off, but was woken early by a
thundering on the door.

Her first thought was that Mitchell Warrender had
come to fling some more unjust accusations in her
direction. Then she realised this was nonsense. She had
her boss on the brain. If he wanted to say anything, he
would wait until she had got to work.

Shrugging into her dressing-gown, Justine turned
the key and peered outside. She still felt drugged with
sleep. Her landlord pushed an envelope into her hand,
muttered a few indistinguishable words, and went
away.

There was no need to puzzle over the contents.
Justine ripped the envelope open and pulled out the
single sheet of paper. It gave her formal notice to quit
the flat within seven days.

Justine's heart dropped. Her landlord had warned
her several times, but she had never thought he would
do it. She was paying her rent, if not the arrears, so
what kind of a monster was he? But it was no use
crying. She was definitely not going back to Gerald
Jamieson. Overnight she had made up her mind
about that. She would find a smaller flat, a bedsit if
necessary, anything so that she could be on her own.

Once she had proved her worth at Warrender's, she
would ask for a raise. Mr Hunt was pleased with her—
he would put in a good word, she was sure. She dared
not think what the big man himself would say. In fact,
she was reluctant to think about Mitchell Warrender
at all.

He had caused her an almost sleepless night and a
great deal of soul-searching. She could not understand
him, nor herself for responding to him when there was
such open animosity between them. The best thing

she could do was to keep out of his way—if that were possible.

But at work she could not hide her anxiety. 'You look as though you've lost a pound and found a penny,' said Fran, one of the other designers with whom she had become friendly.

Justine grimaced. 'I've had notice to quit my flat at the end of the week. I'm so worried! You don't know anywhere reasonable, do you? I can't afford much, not on the pittance they pay here.'

'Pittance?' Fran frowned. 'I always thought they were generous. What are you used to getting—a small fortune?'

In the next few minutes Justine discovered that her salary was half that of the other girl—who was of a similar age and experience. So why the difference?

'Perhaps he's put you on trial?' suggested Fran. 'I know he's had to get rid of one or two who haven't proved up to it. But you're good, and Mr Warrender knows it. I heard Mr Hunt telling him so the other day.'

Justine shrugged. 'It's made no difference—and certainly doesn't help me now.'

'I'll ask around,' said Fran. 'Someone must know of a room. If the worst comes to the worst, I'm sure my mother will put you up until you find somewhere.'

'You're so kind.' Justine had not had much kindness shown her since her mother died and could not thank her new friend enough.

For the rest of the day she lived in constant fear that Mitchell Warrender might send for her. Why, she had no idea. But what he had done to her last night preyed on her mind, and she was sure it was not the end.

She spent the evening sorting out her things. There was nothing else to do, and no point in sitting worrying. But the next morning, Fran told her that she had found a flat.

'It's quite good for the money, and there are two bedrooms, so if you want to ask someone to share it will cut your costs even further.'

'You're an angel,' said Justine. 'How did you manage it?'

'I didn't do anything,' smiled Fran. 'I just let it be known that you were flat-hunting, and one of the directors' secretaries told me about this. I understand a friend of hers has just moved out. We'll go and have a look at lunchtime, if you like?'

It was perfect—one of four flats in a large house in Bayswater. Not so classy as the one she had had, but good enough. There were two small bedrooms, a pokey kitchen and a sitting-room, and Justine would be able to manage the rent easily. In fact, it seemed too good to be true.

At the weekend she moved in, and on Sunday night she had a visitor. He said he was her new landlord.

It was Mitchell Warrender.

Justine was aghast. 'You! How can it be?'

'Why not?' His smile was sinister. He wore a dark suit and looked threatening.

'But why wasn't I told?' Her heart began to flutter like a trapped bird.

'Did you enquire who owned the property?'

'I didn't think it necessary, but if I'd known——'

'You wouldn't have taken it? That's what I thought. May I come in?'

She didn't seem to have any choice, just as she'd had no choice that evening he took her out for a meal. She wondered what he had in mind on this occasion?

He entered the room, and Justine walked across to the other side of it, feeling as though he was sealing her doom when he closed the door. There was nothing except feminine intuition to make her uneasy, and yet she was.

Eyeing him boldly, she said, 'Is it rent you're after?'

hoping it wasn't. She had no money until next pay-day.

'A talk, no more. Shall we sit?' The room boasted two armchairs only, placed directly opposite to each other, and she had no alternative but to take the twin to his.

A warmth stole over her at his nearness. The palpitating beats of her heart changed to a pounding which echoed in her ears, her whole body vibrantly aware of his irrefutable masculinity. He affected her as no other man had before. It was crazy, considering that he hated her and was doing his best to make her hate him.

'You seem to have taken control of my life,' she said. 'First my work, and now my home. Why?'

'Does it disturb you?' The curve to his mouth, the glint of humour in his eye, did not fool her for one second.

'It depends on your reason for doing it.'

'And does there have to be a reason? You came to me for a job, don't forget. Your friend asked my secretary if she knew where there was a flat to let. My role in this is incidental.'

Justine did not believe him for one second. There was a calculating gleam in his eyes. He was doing his best to conceal it, but she was too conscious of his feelings towards her to be deceived.

'So why are you pestering me?' she demanded.

His brows rose in a straight line. 'You did not appear to mind the other evening.'

'It won't happen again. You made it perfectly clear why you made a pass. You found out I was just as responsive as any other girl. Wasn't that enough?' She dared not look at him. The directness of his gaze made her stomach churn. It was an insane situation. She wanted him out of here, yet her body responded. She hoped he wouldn't attempt to touch her.

'You're very attractive, very beautiful. I can see why men find you irresistible.'

'What men?' demanded Justine crossly.

'Any man. You've caused quite a stir since coming to work for me. Don't tell me you're not aware of it?'

'No, I'm not,' she flashed.

'The saying that men prefer blondes is simply not true. Your raven hair and those bright blue eyes are a lethal combination. You're a shade skinny, but you walk tall and there's not one man on the company who would say no to a night out with you.'

'You're making it up.' Justine tilted her chin aggressively and glared at him. 'I'd know if that were the case.'

'Would you? You go around in a daze most of the time—as though you have all the worries of the world on your shoulders.' He leaned forward and touched her hand on the arm of the chair.

Justine snatched it away, feeling as if he had branded her. 'Have you any complaints about my work?'

He shook his head.

'Then it's none of your business.'

'I imagine,' he said slowly, 'that your worries are now over. You have a job, a flat——'

'Neither of my own choice,' she said abruptly. 'I was quite happy where I was, and a whole lot better off financially. My life has been totally disrupted over the last few weeks—and it's still going to be a struggle.'

'Perhaps you've had things too easy?' His eyes never left her face, assessing, awaiting her reaction.

Justine frowned, wondering what he meant. 'I don't think so. I had a good education but I wasn't spoilt. My—father wouldn't allow it.'

'Ah, your father. Don't you find his attitude towards you somewhat odd?'

Justine eyed him warily. 'Not since I found out the reason.'

'Which is?'

She saw no point in refusing to tell him, even though he was taking a more than normal interest. 'He's not my natural father.'

The confession did not surprise him as much as she expected. His eyes merely widened and he said, 'So who is?'

She shrugged. 'That I would like to know.'

'Your mother never told you?'

'No.'

'She doesn't sound much of a lady. Whose name's on the birth certificate?'

A trickle of anger ran through Justine. 'Gerald's— and I'd thank you not to speak about my mother like that. She wasn't a tramp.'

'She remained faithful to her husband? Amazing!' A sneer curled his lips. 'But as he married her to give the baby a name, I suppose she had no choice. She owed him that much.'

Justine took a deep angry breath and pushed herself upright. 'How do you know? You're being pretty insulting, considering you never knew my mother.'

He was quiet for a moment; then he, too, stood up. 'I met your mother,' he said softly, almost menacingly, 'before you, little girl, were born.'

Justine took a step back. What was he saying? How could he have known Delphine?

'You look surprised, as well you might. Delphine was not one of my favourite people. If I'd been a man then, I think I would have killed her. As I was only twelve at the time, I had to be content with promising myself vengeance just as soon as I was old enough.'

'Vengeance for what?' Justine's eyes were two deep puzzled pools of blue. He was talking in riddles.

His nostrils dilated as he stared at her, his face hard

and bitter. 'She tried to con my father that her baby—you—was his. He knew it wasn't, and her attempted deception devastated him. The result was a stroke which left him partially paralysed.' He paused for his words to sink in. 'And since your mother's no longer around, *I intend taking my revenge on you.*'

CHAPTER THREE

JUSTINE stared at Mitchell aghast, her heartbeats echoing loudly in her head, constricting her throat. He wasn't serious? And yet he had never looked more so. A cold sweat stole over her and she began to shake. 'I don't believe you,' she whispered.

'About your mother?' The calculating hardness never left his eyes.

She nodded, trying to swallow, feeling as though she were going to choke.

'It's true, every word of it. Delphine was a scheming little bitch.'

Justine flinched at his acrimonious tones and groped for the chair behind her, her legs no longer able to hold her up. 'No!' she cried, shaking her head wildly. *'No!'*

'Perhaps she kept her bad side from you?' suggested Mitchell maliciously. 'But I can assure you it was there.'

Justine glared at him, her eyes full of pain. 'It's a lie. My mother loved Gerald.'

'Correction. You mother *used* Gerald. He gave her security—the security she tried to get from my father. I couldn't have stood her as a stepmother. But poor Gerald put up with her countless affairs. He was besotted, poor devil. Lord knows what it was she had that made men fall in love with her. Or perhaps I do know, having met you. You have an indefinable something that drives men crazy. Unfortunately, my father never got over her—despite what she did to him.'

Justine felt sick. 'You're lying. You're trying to

discredit her just because you didn't like her. My
mother wasn't like that at all.'

'No?' His brows rose sceptically.

'No!' she cried, 'and I refuse to listen to your
accusations. Your mind's diseased. You're making the
whole thing up just because you've found out who I
am.'

'Would I make up anything like that? It's your
mother's mind that was sick.'

'If you believe that, then your father was no saint
either for having an affair with her.'

His eyes grew icy, his jaw once again firm and
resolute. 'It was no casual affair, at least not on my
father's side. My mother had been dead three years.
Delphine was the first woman he looked at afterwards.'

'And she led him on? Is that what you're implying?'
demanded Justine hotly. 'There's no blame at all on
your father's side. He's too perfect for words.'

'That's enough!' Mitchell's eyes were blazing.
'Don't speak about my father like that.'

'I see,' she shot back. 'You're allowed to slander my
mother because she's not alive to defend herself, but
no one must breathe a word about your parent. How
one-sided can you get?'

'My father was a fool, I'll admit.' His voice had the
chill of a winter morning. 'But in his own way he
loved Delphine. She was as opposite from my mother
as it is possible for two people to be. Perhaps that was
the attraction. It was a different love—no one could
ever take my mother's place.'

'But apparently he did not love her enough to marry
her when she became pregnant?' Justine challenged,
wondering what it would have been like having this
man as a stepbrother. A fate worse than death, from
what she had seen of him so far.

A pulse jerked in his jaw. 'He would have done if

she hadn't tried to insist the baby was his. Delphine had never shown that side of her character before.'

'And how did he know it wasn't his baby if he was going to bed with her?' pounded Justine ferociously.

'Because——' he said, with renewed grimness '—my father is sterile.'

'You're lying,' she snapped. 'Your father didn't want to own up to his responsibilities, that's the top and bottom of it.'

He held her gaze, his hostility coming between them like a brick wall. 'It's the truth. My father's never been able to have children. I was adopted—but I've always loved my parents as if they were my own flesh and blood, and I'm prepared to go to any lengths to wreak vengeance on their behalf.'

Pausing, he heaved a grim sigh. 'He's always had high blood pressure. He had a mild heart attack when my mother died. And the shock about the baby, especially when Delphine told him she had never loved him, that she was merely after a rich husband—oh, she rubbed it in all right—did permanent damage.'

Justine felt chilled right through to her marrow. It was such an unpleasant picture he painted, it could not possibly be true. Delphine would never do such a thing! Admittedly, she had stayed away from home often—but visiting girlfriends, not other men. Mitchell was making it up to justify his treatment of her daughter. He was a sadistic brute, and she hated him.

'You're a liar. I'll never believe you, not in a thousand years,' she declared.

The granite hardness of his eyes pierced her like a knife. There was a fearsome stillness about him, his whole body rigid with an emotion too frightening to think about. He carried on speaking as though he hadn't heard her.

'The consequences of your mother's action are a constant reminder of her vile deed. My father recovered to a certain extent, but when he tried to take up the reins of his business again, it was too much. Another heart attack followed, and his doctor said that if he did not take things easy he would be a dead man. By the time I was old enough to take over, things were pretty grim. There was almost no Warrender's Shoes. The new M.D. hadn't the same initiative as my father. It's been a long hard haul back to the top—and I shall never forget why it happened.'

'But your father's last attack might have happened anyway,' said Justine hoarsely. 'You're insane if you're blaming my mother for all this.'

'I don't think so.' His eyes gleamed with an odd light. 'It's been a long time, but now it's going to give me the greatest pleasure to make you pay.' He pushed himself up and towered above her.

She shrank back into her seat, her eyes wide and fearful. 'You can't possibly take it out on me for something you only think my mother did.'

'I don't think, I know,' he growled, 'and my revenge won't be anything physical. I just intend seeing that you don't get a moment's peace.' With one last searing look, he swung on his heel and left the room.

Justine felt as though he had delivered her a sledge-hammer blow. It was her mother all along he had been comparing her with, trying to find out whether she was as free with her body as he claimed Delphine had been. But it couldn't possibly be true—could it? Her mother would never have tried to palm off someone else's child as the elder Mr Warrender's. Mitchell had got it wrong. He had been a child when it happened, and over the years the incident had grown out of all proportion in his mind until he had difficulty in distinguishing between fact and fiction. She could not believe he intended persecuting her for what must be all in his mind. It was monstrous.

Too stunned to move, she remained in the chair.

Over the past few weeks her whole life had been turned upside down, and all by this man.

By this man!

That was it! Everything became suddenly clear. He was behind her dismissal, everything. It was he who had spread the vicious lies, and who would dare disbelieve a man like Mitchell Warrender?

Shocked to the core, Justine sprang up, her heart banging inside her ribcage. He had planned this all along. First she lost her job, then her flat, and both times *he* came to her rescue.

How much had he paid her landlord to get rid of her? She had wondered why the man was so hard-hearted after she managed to find another job. Now she knew. The feeling of hatred was definitely mutual now, and she cringed when she thought how readily she had responded to Mitchell Warrender's advances.

But if this desire to avenge had grown and festered over the past twenty-four years, it must be fearsome indeed, and didn't augur well for her own future. She wondered why Mitchell had never contacted her mother. Wasn't it her he should have tackled?

Perhaps he'd been too busy building up the family business. It was only now that he had the time, the wealth, and the power to do something about it. And she was taking her mother's place!

Justine went to bed, but her mind was too active to let her sleep, and she was fully aware that if Mitchell Warrender carried out his threat she would have many more sleepless nights to follow.

Next morning it was work as usual. Had she had a choice Justine would never have gone there again, but running away from her problem would not solve it. In fact, by not turning up she would play right into Mitchell's hands. She would be out of a job and a home before she knew it.

She expected to see him, expected him to call her to

his office on some trumped-up excuse, but the whole day passed without her even catching sight of him.

He was in the building, she knew, and she was on tenterhooks the whole time, so nervy and jumpy that Mr Hunt asked more than once what was wrong. Fran, too, enquired whether she was feeling well.

'It's the flat,' countered Justine. 'I wish I hadn't taken it. I don't feel happy there.'

'But you only moved in a couple of days ago. How can you say that?'

'It's just a feeling,' she shrugged. 'I expect it will pass.'

She wished she could confide in someone, but it was such a ridiculous story no one would believe her. No one at Warrender's ever had a bad word to say for the head of the company. There was speculation as to why he had never married, but most people put it down to the fact that he was never in one spot long enough to form a permanent relationship.

He jetted all over the world, keeping a keen eye on his envied chain of shops and factories, and someone had said only the other day that they had never known him stay in London so long.

If they knew why, she would become the talking point of the whole place. How she wished she had never taken the job! She ought to have moved right away from London when the first hint of disaster made itself felt. Left the country, even. He would never have found her then.

Had she known about Mitchell Warrender and his plans for vengeance she would have gone. Her mistake had been in staying in the same area once her name was smeared. He had certainly done a good job in that direction. Not one person had been prepared to take her on. She was black-listed probably right across the country.

At six o'clock Justine did not know whether to

breathe a sigh of relief or not. It was possible Mitchell Warrender would turn up at the flat again—in fact, since he had not spoken to her all day, that was probably what he had in mind.

She would have eaten out if she could have afforded to, and not returned until bedtime, but as things stood she went straight home and locked the door, determined not to open it to anyone. He couldn't force his way in. She would call the police if he tried.

But she worried for nothing. There was no sign of him all evening and she went to bed with a surprising sense of anti-climax.

The next few days followed the same pattern, and his cat and mouse game began to prey on Justine's nerves. He had vowed not to let her have one moment's peace, so where was he? What was he doing?

A whole week went by before she saw him again. On Saturday morning she opened her door and he was there, almost as though he had stood waiting outside, and Justine felt the colour drain from her face. He had lulled her into a false sense of security. For the first time she had not checked from her window to see whether his car was outside.

'Good morning, Justine.'

There was nothing in his tone to suggest this was not a friendly visit. Any observer would see a tall, good-looking man dressed casually in grey slacks and a navy blazer. They would probably think that she was lucky that such an attractive member of the male sex was visiting her.

The only luck that entered into it was bad luck— with capital letters. She held on to the door handle. 'What do you want?'

'Now, there's a greeting! I've come to take you out for the day.' His smile was perfectly friendly, even reaching the smoky grey of his eyes.

Justine immediately grew suspicious. What devious

plan had he in mind now? He was not inviting her out
of the goodness of his heart, that was for sure. 'No
thanks, I have things to do.'

'Forget them.' The injunction was short and sharp.

'How can I? Weekends are the only time when I can
shop and clean and do my washing.'

'You can shop while we are out. Anything else will
have to wait.'

He certainly liked giving his orders. Justine
wondered whether she dared protest further. She
certainly had no wish to spend a day in the company
of Mitchell Warrender. It went without saying that it
would be neither happy nor successful.

Her hesitation irritated him. A scowl appeared and
he said sharply, 'Now what's wrong?'

Justine glanced down at the green velour pants and
delicate lacy white sweater which outlined her model-
girl figure, resigned already to the fact that she had no
choice. 'I'm wondering whether I ought to change.'

'Into something less provocative.' His eyes insolently
assessed her firm pointed breasts, lingering far longer
than necessary, causing a faint quickening of her pulses.

Alarm raced through her. How could she possibly
still be affected by him? He was her enemy. Never
again would she allow him to get close—not in a
physical sense. It was far too dangerous.

'You look all right just as you are. You have
excellent taste, if I may say so—inherited, I imagine,
from your mother. She was always beautifully dressed.
Even as a boy I saw that.' Speaking about Delphine
brought a sudden grimness to his mouth, and he
turned abruptly. 'Let's go.'

Justine felt the same bitterness. They would never
see eye to eye where her mother was concerned. But
for the moment she would keep her thoughts to
herself. There was no point in spoiling the day before
it started.

She sank into the luxury of his car, smelling leather and aftershave, and feeling an extraordinary, disturbing sense of intimacy.

Her awareness of him increased by the second, and she wished she'd had the strength to refuse the invitation. Their meetings always ended in disaster, and this one would be no exception. In fact, after the insinuations he had made the other night, she could not see their ever being remotely friendly.

He drove out of the city, joined the motorway, and headed towards the coast. The silence became unbearable, making Justine wonder why he had opted to take her out.

At length he spoke. 'Your mother never remained silent for this long. From what I remember, she constantly chattered.'

Justine looked at him contemptuously. 'I'm not my mother.'

'But you are of her blood.'

'And that is supposed to make us the same?' Her blue eyes flashed, her tone became aggressive. 'I'm furious when I recall what you said. I don't believe a word, but nevertheless you've caused me many sleepless nights.'

'Good!' His hard grey eyes caught and held hers for a fraction of time. 'That was my intention.'

'And today you're going to carry on the persecution? You don't care that you've got the whole thing wrong?' She flung the words bitterly across the space between them, wishing they were a hundred miles apart instead of only a few inches.

'Today I'm going to get to know you better.' The smile which accompanied his words was anything but friendly. In fact, Justine saw it as a threat and made a vow there and then to maintain a discreet distance.

But this was not easy. They reached the coast in no

time at all and he took her to a deserted cove,
surprisingly not far from Brighton.

He smiled wickedly at her expression and pointed to
a beach-house hanging precariously on the cliff-side
above them. 'That belongs to a friend of mine. This is
a private beach. We shan't be disturbed.'

'I'm glad to hear it,' she said drily, watching as he
spread a blanket on the fine dry sand, dropping a
picnic basket on one corner and then motioning her to
sit. Eyeing him uneasily, Justine did so. A picnic was
the last thing she had expected. Picnics were happy
occasions, enjoyed by all who took part, but there was
no pleasure in sharing an outing with this man.

He joined her and they sat side by side, leaning back
on their hands and looking out at the English Channel.
The water was green this sunny summer morning, and
inviting. Justine wished he had told her his plans; she
would have enjoyed a swim.

'Tell me what you're thinking.'

She turned to discover Mitchell watching her, his
eyes searching her face. His animosity seemed to have
gone. Whether this was deliberate or not, she did not
know.

There was something disturbingly intimate about
the way he scrutinised each of her features in turn—
her eyes, her nose, mouth, cheeks, hair—and she
wondered whether he was still comparing her with her
mother.

And yet the hardness that turned his face into a
chiselled mask when he thought of Delphine was
missing. He must see Justine as a separate individual,
as a person in her own right. Her cheeks grew warm
and she dropped her eyes.

A prickly heat bathed her skin and her heartbeat
increased alarmingly. These were feelings over which
she had no control, despite her aversion. There were
times when she hated the sight of him and others, like

now, when he had only to look at her and her bones seemed to melt.

'I was thinking I'd like to swim,' she said. 'I wish you'd told me what you had in mind.'

'Would you have brought your swimsuit if I had?' he countered with a smile.

'I suppose not,' admitted Justine.

'There's nothing to stop you swimming in the nude.' A challenge gleamed in his eyes, and his lips curved mockingly.

'Except my inherent sense of modesty,' she returned quietly.

'Would you do it if you loved me?' he demanded, a glint of something she could not understand in his eyes.

'That would be different,' she acknowledged. 'But as it's never likely to be the case, I see no point in the question.'

'I agree it's hypothetical,' he said, 'but I want to find out the way your mind works.'

'You mean you're wondering whether I'm as promiscuous as you suggest my mother was?' Justine held herself stiffly erect, challenging him with beautiful eyes that seemed a reflection of the sky overhead.

His lips quirked. 'I must admit there is a difference—but you're forgetting, I don't know you very well—not yet, that is. You could be putting on an act for my benefit. Delphine was expert at that sort of thing.'

Justine tossed her head, a welcome breeze whipping her short dark hair across her face. 'Please don't talk about my mother like that.'

'You think I'm making it up?' His eyes locked with her own in silent challenge.

So strong was his magnetism that Justine could not look away, even though she wanted to. His deepset

smoky grey eyes were narrowed slightly at this
moment, sending her signals that she chose to ignore.
The whites were very clear, his lashes thick and dark.
They were the most beautiful eyes she had ever seen
on a man.

Emotions she tried hard to suppress leapt into
action, surging along her nerve-streams until she felt
as though she were electrically alive. If he touched her
sparks would fly, she was sure.

It annoyed her that she was not strong enough to
withstand his sex appeal. This was a man she should
hate, should be wary of; a man she told herself she *did*
hate—and yet her response when they were together
like this was total.

He had proved it that first time he took her out and
she invited him back to her flat. She had been unable
to help herself, her whole body willingly accepting
what she thought he offered, never dreaming for one
moment that he was testing her.

'I'm sure of it,' she said, deliberately hardening her
voice. 'But if you've made up your mind to punish
me—for the sake of some ridiculous story you've
concocted about my mother—then I've no doubt
you'll do exactly that.'

With a supreme effort she dragged her eyes away,
but a second later a firm hand touched her chin,
compelling her once again to meet his dark gaze. His
fingers remained to torment her, his thumb stroking
her chin in a soft caress. 'Let's just get one thing clear:
I do not tell lies. What I have told you is the truth.'

'Then prove it,' snapped Justine.

He smiled maliciously. 'You think I can't?'

'I know you can't,' she retorted, and still his fingers
remained. Justine knew his touch was expertly
designed to arouse her baser instincts, despite their
conflict. It was fortunate he could not see the emotions
inside her—for they would have been a dead giveaway.

How ironic that she could not help herself where this man was concerned. But she gave no outward show of being affected, eyeing him stonily, waiting for him to release her.

He gave a secret smile and let his hand drop. She was sure it was no accident that it brushed her breast. Her pulses leapt and her inner excitement, fuelled by her anger, increased, but still she maintained an indifferent façade.

'Let's swim,' he said with an abrupt change of tone, 'and if you're too modest to strip off in front of me, then we'll have to find you something to wear.'

Guardedly, Justine eyed him. 'Don't tell me you packed a swimsuit on the offchance?' Not that she would put anything past him.

'No, but my friend up there——' raising his eyes towards the beach-house '—will definitely have something to fit you.'

'Your friend is female?' Justine did not know why, but she had assumed the house belonged to a man. She should have known better. Mitchell Warrender was hardly the type to cultivate male friendships.

'Naturally.' He sprang up and held out his hand. 'It's a heck of a climb, but worth it. Up there you feel as though you're on top of the world.'

Justine ignored his hand, missing his frown as she picked up her bag. 'Will this stuff be safe?'

He nodded, 'Don't worry about it,' and led the way to where a series of steps had been hewn into the cliff-face. A rusting iron rail gave scant protection from the fierce drop below and Justine kept close to Mitchell as they ascended.

His powerful legs climbed effortlessly, and she had no doubt that he could go all the way to the top without a break. But halfway he turned and, observing her laboured breathing and the beads of perspiration on her brow, suggested she might like a rest.

'Yes, please,' said Justine at once, testing the rail before she leaned back against it. Her breasts rose and fell, straining against the lacy fabric of her sweater. Her cheeks were flushed, her eyes bright, and she looked very beautiful.

Mitchell surveyed her lazily, his breathing hardly any deeper than normal. 'You're out of condition. Do you take part in any sports?'

'Not really,' said Justine, shaking her head. 'I used to play squash with my brother, but since I've lived on my own and made new friends, I haven't bothered.'

'None of them is very athletic?'

'No.' Actually most of her girlfriends were now married or courting, and as she didn't like going anywhere on her own she had tended to stay in a lot, especially when money became short after her sacking.

'You ought to do something,' he said. 'My father spent too much time working and not exercising, and look where it got him. I vowed never to make the same mistake. I try to keep myself at the peak of physical fitness.'

There was no answer Justine could give to that. His superb body was living proof. 'I think I'm ready to go on,' she said.

'Are you sure?' His dark eyes rested on her still-heaving breasts, bringing a tingling awareness to them.

Justine pushed past him. 'Of course I am.' He had no right to disturb her like this.

His hand shot out and grabbed her arm. For an instant she felt his tremendous strength, and then just as suddenly, he let her go. But not before his eyes had read the truth in hers. He knew exactly how much he disturbed her.

She led the way this time, climbing the steep steps with difficulty, her legs beginning to feel like rubber. Had Mitchell not been behind her she would have rested again, but she was determined not to let him see her weaken.

At the very top she stopped and turned, and he caught her as her legs buckled, holding her hard against his firm chest. Justine clung to him limply, thankful, for once, for his presence.

'Well done!'

Praise indeed. Justine lifted her head and looked at him. 'As you said, it was quite a climb. I hadn't realised.' She felt the thump of his heart, so much slower and controlled than her own, felt the sheer strength and magnetism of him, and struggled to escape.

He let her go, smiling enigmatically. 'Sure you can stand?'

Vigorously Justine nodded. There was something different about Mitchell up here. He was no longer her boss, or the hard man seeking vengeance. He seemed to be making an effort to be friendly, and she ought to respond.

Yet how did she know he was to be trusted? Maybe he was luring her into a false sense of security? There was no way of knowing exactly what thoughts went through his head.

'Right, let's set about finding you that swimsuit.' He strode towards the grey stone house, perfectly familiar with his surroundings.

Justine looked after him. The sea-facing wall was made almost entirely of glass, fronted with a balcony on which stood a white-painted table and chairs painted white.

It looked extremely tempting and she could imagine herself sitting there, looking out to sea. It would be wonderfully relaxing.

'Are you coming?' Mitchell's voice broke into her thoughts.

She smiled and walked towards him. 'What a beautiful place.'

'At the moment, but it can be pretty bleak in winter. Pru uses it as a holiday home, that's all.'

'And she's not here now?'

He shook his head. 'She's somewhere in the Caribbean, topping up her tan. She adores the sun.

'And she lets you use it whenever you like?'

He grinned. 'I have an open invitation. Not that I take her up on it often. I'm far too busy. But it's useful if I feel like the odd day away from it all. Actually, I try to avoid London as much as possible. It's not one of my favourite places.'

Which meant he was there because of her! Justine compressed her lips as she watched him select the right key from his ring.

Once inside she could not wait to find the room with the view. It was as fantastic as she had imagined. Mitchell slid open the glass doors and they stepped out on to the balcony. It was indeed like being on top of the world.

The cliffs fell steeply away, giving wide un-interrupted views of the Channel. Puffy white clouds marred the horizon, spoiling what up till now had been a cloudless sky. Somewhere out there was France. Gulls wheeled and screamed overhead. They were alone with the elements. And she was alone with Mitchell. At his mercy if he decided to take advantage of the situation.

Glancing across, Justine was surprised to see him watching her. She had thought he too was admiring the view. There was an unnerving, speculative gleam in his eyes. She attempted a smile. 'I've never been anywhere quite so isolated.'

'It's pretty startling first time around,' he agreed. 'It depends on the type of person you are. I imagine that you, like your mother, prefer crowds. You wouldn't be happy here for long.'

'I wish you wouldn't keep comparing us,' said

Justine crossly. 'We may look alike, but there the likeness ends. I quite enjoy being on my own.'

'So you do admit that your mother enjoyed the company of others?'

'She had girlfriends, yes,' said Justine.

His brows slid up but he made no comment. Nor was one needed. She knew what he was thinking.

'Maybe you take after your father? Have you ever wondered who he might be?'

'Frequently,' admitted Justine, 'but if he cared so little about my mother that he let her marry someone else, then I don't think I want to know him.'

'Admirable sentiments.' He still kept a watchful eye on her. 'Was it very much of a shock when Gerald made his monumental announcement?'

Justine thought for a moment. 'A shock, yes; a disappointment, no. Gerald and I never got on. If it hadn't been for my mother, I'd probably have left home years earlier. We were close.'

Suddenly she shivered. The light wind that had been welcome earlier was gaining in strength, whipping the sea into white-crested waves, speeding the clouds across a darkening sky. A typically English weather change, all in a matter of minutes.

'Looks like rain,' said Mitchell matter-of-factly. 'You go inside, I'll dash down and rescue the picnic hamper. We'll eat here instead.' Seconds later she saw him disappear down the steps, not afraid of her running away because there was nowhere to go.

As she watched plump raindrops slide down the window, Justine wondered exactly what his motive was in bringing her here. To get to know her better, he had said. But was that necessary if all he wanted was to avenge his father's reputed callous treatment by her mother?

Whatever he had in mind, why didn't he get it over with? He had already cost her her job and had her thrown out of her lodgings. Why keep her in this constant state of suspense?

He was a long time coming back, but just as she began to fear that he might have left her, Justine heard his car. He had driven round and up the hill, and had now parked at the front of the bungalow.

'There's a storm brewing,' he smiled, as a gust of wind followed him in. 'It looks as though we might be stuck here for several hours.'

'You needn't look so pleased,' said Justine crossly.

'The idea doesn't appeal?'

'Not in the slightest,' she returned, with as much dignity as she could muster. 'Don't forget I didn't want to come in the first place.'

'That's right,' he said. 'But I'm sure I haven't given you any reason to complain.'

'Not yet,' she returned hotly. 'But you must have some devious plan tucked away in the back of your mind—and before the day is over, I shall know what it is.'

'You don't believe that all I want to do is talk?' His eyes widened, a mocking lift to his brows. A picture of perfect innocence.

But Justine was not fooled. 'No!'

'You don't believe that if I get to know you better, I might change my mind about seeking vengeance?'

Justine faced him squarely, her blue eyes intent on his face. 'If I could think that, Mr Warrender, I would willingly spend the rest of the weekend with you.'

The moment she uttered the words, she knew she had made a mistake. A gleam lightened Mitchell's eyes, and he held out his hand. 'Miss Jamieson, you have a deal.'

CHAPTER FOUR

JUSTINE ignored Mitchell's outstretched hand and turned away. 'I shouldn't have said that.' Her voice was almost inaudible.

'But you did, and I have no intention of letting you go back on your word.' He spun her to face him, hard fingers digging into her shoulders.

Triumph glittered in his eyes and a wave of panic washed over Justine. Why, oh why, hadn't she thought before she spoke? 'I can't,' she said huskily. 'I can't do it.'

'Not if it means I leave you alone in future?' The smile that accompanied his question was meant to allay her fears, but Justine read it differently. She would never, ever, believe anything this man said. He was merely taking advantage of the situation.

'You don't fool me that easily,' she spat. 'You'll take whatever you want, and then it will be back to square one. I'll never be free of you. You'll harass me for the rest of my life.'

His eyes narrowed, emitting a cold, fierce light. 'You could be right. It all depends on how this weekend turns out. The result will be entirely up to you.'

How? she wanted to ask. What did she have to do to make sure he never pestered her again? But she knew she would get no positive answer to her questions, so she merely held his gaze, chin high, no sign of her inner panic on her face.

He smiled and let her go, opening the picnic basket and placing the contents on the table. Justine had to admit he'd thought of everything, even down to a bottle of wine.

And so as the heavens were split by jagged streaks of lightning, as heavy black clouds rolled and rumbled ever nearer, they ate a feast fit for a king: avocado and shrimp quiche, jellied chicken, game pâté, crusty rolls, mixed salad and cheeses, fresh fruit. Justine could not fault his choice.

'May I ask who prepared all this?' she ventured, nibbling on a celery stick.

'My father's housekeeper. She's a treasure.'

'Your father still lives in London?' Justine did not know why, but she thought he had moved once he was no longer capable of running the business.

Mitchell nodded. 'He'll never leave. Unlike me, he loves it there. He has a beautiful house just near Regent's Park.'

'And do you stay with him when you're in London?'

'Of course. He sees little enough of me these days. I couldn't disappoint him and book into a hotel.'

'Don't you have a place of your own?'

'What is this, an inquisition? I'm here to find out about you, not the other way around.' But he smiled as he spoke, and Justine knew he was not annoyed.

In fact, the longer she spent with him, the more he seemed to mellow. With a bit of luck, by the end of the day he would have relented enough to take her home.

The next second these hopes were dashed. 'We must go shopping later. Pru always keeps a good stock of basics, but we shall need something for tomorrow's lunch. Are you a good cook?'

'Fair, I suppose.' She wondered what he would say if she said no. Her mother had been the world's worst. Gerald employed a very efficient housekeeper and Delphine had been content to leave things to her. Justine had grown used to this other woman looking after them and it had never occurred to her that her mother might not like housework. She had assumed the reason her mother did nothing was that they were rich enough to pay someone else.

'I'll risk it,' he said, refilling their wine glasses.

It grew darker by the minute, the room lit now only by silver streaks of lightning, each followed by an almost instantaneous roll of thunder.

Justine did not like storms. As a child she had always hidden whenever there was thunder and lightning. Now she tried to hide her fear, concentrating instead on the delightful meal.

But when a particularly loud clap of thunder seemed to shake the very foundations of the house, she could not contain a cry of fear.

Mitchell pushed back his chair and stood up, walking round to her side of the table. 'You're afraid?'

She looked at him and nodded, and he held out a hand. This time she did not ignore the gesture, taking it gladly, grateful for some small measure of comfort.

He drew her across the room and they sat in a corner of the settee, his arm protectively about her shoulders, her head on his chest. Justine could not imagine why he was being nice to her. It did not go with the image he had earlier projected. It would have been more in keeping if he had revelled in her unease, even added in some obscure way to her suffering. But she was not going to worry about that now. Comfort was what she needed, and he was certainly providing that.

For a further fifteen minutes, the savage summer storm raged. Mitchell stroked her hair and murmured soothingly, and it occurred to Justine that if she had him by her side for ever she would never be afraid of storms again.

Gradually it faded into the distance. Justine began to relax, to become aware of Mitchell as the virile man he was, and struggled to free herself.

'What's your hurry?' His voice was a deep husky growl, his arm tight about her.

Justine stiffened. 'The storm's almost over.'

The sky out to sea had recovered its brilliant blue, only a faint clap of thunder could still be heard. It was difficult to believe how fierce the whole thing had been.

'Why move? You feel good in my arms—and I'm sure you're enjoying it.'

She glanced at him suspiciously. What was this, another attempt to class her with Delphine? She did not trust this man one inch. He would never take her at face value; always he would compare her with his memories of her mother.

'I don't think I could ever enjoy being in your arms, Mr Warrender. Thank you for looking after me, but I'm all right again now.'

He scowled. 'What goes with this Mr Warrender business? We're not at work. Call me Mitchell.'

'Please, Mitchell,' said Justine obediently, 'will you let me go?'

'In good time,' he said lazily. 'I'm quite sure you didn't mean that about not liking my company. I've never yet met a woman who's wanted to escape before I've finished with her.'

'Maybe you haven't threatened anyone else,' said Justine positively.

'Do you feel threatened now?' He stroked back a strand of hair from her face, and it felt as though he was searing her skin.

'Very much so,' she announced loudly, denying even to herself that her quickened pulses had anything to do with his nearness. 'You're trying to prove I'm the type of girl you want me to be.'

A slow smile curved his lips. 'You're very smart, but it's the truth, you do feel good. If it wasn't for your—er—unfortunate background, I might feel differently about you.'

Justine increased her struggles. 'Since there's no chance of that, why keep me here against my will?'

'Why indeed?' He put a hand beneath her breast. 'Your heart's fluttering like a frightened bird. Are you afraid of me?'

She lifted brilliant blue eyes to his face, catching her breath at the raw desire she saw there, wishing again they had met under different circumstances. Whether he was seeking vengeance or not, he was taking no pains to hide his arousal and it gave her a feeling of power that she was able to do this to him, despite his hatred. Physical hunger was a very strong emotion. She felt a similar craving herself.

'I'm not afraid of you, Mitchell,' she said evenly. 'It's the storm that's affected me.'

'The storm is over.'

But not inside her. There a storm of a different kind raged, of new and unwanted emotions which she must keep strictly under control. 'It takes me a little while to settle down. I wouldn't mind a cup of coffee, if there is any?'

His arms relaxed and Justine stood up, glancing down at him as she moved away. His eyes were on her still, narrowed speculatively, sending fresh tingles through her spine. Then he pushed himself up and moved through into the kitchen.

Justine busied herself clearing away the remains of their meal, stacking the plates ready for washing, and then joined Mitchell.

The kitchen was small but well-equipped and he already had coffee percolating. She put the plates in the sink and turned on the tap.

'No hot water,' he said. 'I've just switched on the heater. Leave them until later.'

'Can I help with the coffee, then?'

He shook his head. 'Make yourself comfortable on the balcony. I'll bring it out in a minute.'

Justine did not need telling twice. She slid open the heavy glass door, inhaling appreciatively. The rain had released fresh odours, the roses and marigolds in the minuscule garden were refreshed and bright. The whole scene was like a newly painted picture. But the table and chairs were dewed with raindrops, so she went back indoors for a cloth.

She met Mitchell at the kitchen door, the loaded tray in his hands. He did not hear her, nor she him, and their resultant collision sent the pot of coffee flying.

'Oh, Lord, I'm sorry,' he said at once. 'I had no idea you were there.'

Justine was soaked and held her sweater away from her smarting skin.

'You'd better strip off quickly,' said Mitchell. 'Pru's bedroom's there,' nodding to a door the other side of the hall. 'Can I help?'

Justine shook her head vigorously. Her skin tingled where the hot coffee had touched and she wanted to tear her clothes off there and then, but she waited until she was decently inside.

Her bra was wet too, and her skin glowed red. Mitchell tapped on the door. Justine glanced hurriedly around for a robe to make herself decent.

'Justine, I have a tube of ointment here especially for burns and scalds. Do you mind if I come in?'

'Yes, I do,' she yelled, madly opening wardrobes, but it made no difference because the door was already open.

A pair of white lacy briefs was her only protection against his all-seeing eyes. She tried to pretend there was nothing unusual in his seeing her almost naked, and held out her hand for the ointment.

'I'll take a shower first,' she said, 'if there is one. I feel kind of sticky.'

'And sore, too, I imagine.'

'No thanks to you,' she snapped, taking refuge in anger even though she knew the fault was as much hers.

His face hardened. 'I have apologised. You don't think I did it deliberately? I thought you were out on the balcony.'

'And I thought you were still making coffee.' She strode past him. 'If you won't show me where the bathroom is, I'll find it myself.'

He grinned and moved quickly into the hall, pushing open the next door. 'Here we are. I think you should find all you need. If not, give me a shout.'

The shower was already hot, but the warm water increased Justine's discomfort and she let it run cold, standing beneath the fine jets until all the tingling soreness had gone and she ached with cold instead.

A towelling robe hung behind the door and she wrapped it around her, forgetting her burns until the coarse material rubbed them.

She ran into the bedroom, letting the robe fall, then she smoothed on the ointment before pulling a soft cheesecloth shirt over her head. It was mid-thigh length and looked good even without trousers.

Whoever Pru might be, Justine was grateful that her clothes fitted. She brushed her hair and then rinsed out her jumper and trousers, pegging them out on a line near the back door.

When she joined Mitchell on the balcony, he was half reclining, his feet resting on the balustrade, eyes closed. Justine sat down and poured herself a cup of coffee from the fresh pot he had made, sprinkling it with sugar but ignoring the powdered milk.

She looked up to find him watching her. It was a habit of his, and he always caught her off guard. She smiled self-consciously and said, 'I feel much better now.'

'You look it,' he returned. 'I hate women in trousers. Legs were made to be looked at.'

Instantly she wished she had chosen something with a bit more coverage; she did not relish the idea of his ogling her. But at least she could be grateful that she had good legs and a passable tan.

Tucking them neatly beneath her chair, she sipped her coffee. 'Trousers are practical. I wear them often.'

'If you were my woman, you wouldn't,' he growled.

Justine knew he was baiting her so said nothing. It was a pointless statement. He was playing with her, teasing her as a cat does a mouse, and at any moment would move in to make his kill.

'We'll give our lunch an hour or so to go down, and then have that swim,' he said, 'or doesn't the idea appeal any more?'

Already Justine's scald was beginning to burn again—seawater would be the perfect antidote. 'I'd love it. Can't we go now?' Anything would be preferable to sitting here. Mitchell Warrender was proving irresistible. Before she knew what was happening, she would end up liking him!

'Didn't your mother ever tell you that swimming after a meal was bad for you?'

Justine shrugged. 'She probably didn't know. She wasn't a swimmer. In fact, not the sporty type at all.'

'Except when the game was a man?' he thrust.

He had full sensual lips and Justine hated it when he clamped them together. It made him look menacing—and he only ever did it when he talked about Delphine.

It seemed impossible to hold a conversation without her mother coming into it. Despite the fact that she was dead, she dominated their relationship. 'Here we go again,' she cried bitterly. 'Aren't you ever going to let up?'

His eyes widened. 'I speak only the truth. If it hurts, that's not my fault.'

'The truth as you see it,' shot back Justine. 'Your eyes are so blinkered you wouldn't see the real truth if it stared you in the face.'

'You're so much like her,' he continued smoothly. 'Is it any wonder I feel as I do?'

She ought to have known he'd have an answer every time. 'I only look like her,' she protested. Their temperaments had been totally different: Delphine enjoying a good time and the bright lights; Justine much more serious. Nevertheless, Delphine had done her best to be a good mother.

He shrugged lazily. 'You're right, but it doesn't alter the fact. However, since you find the subject so unpleasant, we'll change it.'

'I don't find talking about my mother unpleasant,' she cried angrily, 'only when you belittle her.'

'So you still think she was a paragon of virtue?'

A sneer curled his lip, making Justine see red. 'Compared to you, she was a saint,' she raged. 'I never heard her run anyone down—and that's all you've done since I met you.'

'With just cause,' he grated, shooting suddenly to his feet, knocking the table as he did so and almost causing the second lot of coffee to crash to the floor. 'When you're ready, I'll meet you on the beach.'

Justine closed her eyes and let out a deep sigh. Arguing with Mitchell took so much out of her. It was impossible to relax when he was around.

But the sun's rays were soothing and soporific and before she knew it she was asleep, not waking until she heard a loud bellow from the beach below.

Struggling to open her eyes, she saw Mitchell looking up at her, arms akimbo, a pair of white swimming trunks taut across his loins. Even from this distance it was impossible not to see the full muscular strength of him.

She stood up and waved, then went indoors and

changed into one of Pru's minuscule bikinis. They each looked as though they were held in place by will-power, and were far more daring than any Justine normally wore.

Descending the steps with care, she found Mitchell waiting for her at the bottom. His eyes, as usual, made their own appraisal of her body. She was getting used to his bold assessments, but it did not make them any easier to accept. He looked at her as though the strips of scarlet material were non-existent, eyeing her curves with an insolence she found degrading.

Without bothering to speak, Justine swung away and ran across the sand towards the glittering sea. Mitchell's feet pounded behind her and they entered the water together, wading for the first few yards and then plunging into the icy depths.

And it was icy! Justine gasped as she surfaced, facing a chuckling Mitchell, who had been in the water already that afternoon.

'Why didn't you warn me? It's freezing!' She wrapped her arms about her shoulders, her teeth chattering.

'It's invigorating. Come on, you coward, you'll soon get used to it. What were you doing up there that took you so long?'

'I went to sleep,' admitted Justine ruefully.

'Well, this will certainly wake you.' He scooped a handful of water and threw it over her.

She retaliated, and they spent the next few minutes fooling around. Then they swam out for a hundred yards and back again, Justine doing her best to keep up with him.

'You're a good swimmer.' The compliment was freely given when they finally waded ashore, and he wrapped a towel about her before rubbing himself vigorously with another.

Justine felt wonderfully, vitally alive and wished

Mitchell was always such fun. When he forgot who she was, he was a perfect companion. Lucky the girl who married him!

They lay down on their towels, eyes closed against the sun, Justine pulsingly aware of the virile specimen beside her. Whether he slept, she did not know.

Then it was time to scale the cliff-face again. The steps did not seem so steep. Whether the swim had put a new life into her or whether it was her heightened awareness of Mitchell, Justine did not know. Whatever, she felt on top of the world, almost as though she could run to the top. But the steps were too steep for that, and when she did reach the bungalow, her legs ached so much she was glad to sit down.

'I think you ought to shower again before you get too comfortable,' suggested Mitchell. 'Wash off the salt. I'll follow.'

She shook her head. 'You go first. I'm exhausted. I can't move an inch.'

'I'm not surprised,' he laughed. 'You flew up those steps like a veteran. I wondered what had got into you.'

She smiled secretly and, letting her head drop back, closed her eyes. 'Call me when the shower's free.'

It was blissful lying back on a lounger. She felt good, better than she had in a long time—and it was all because of this man. A man she should hate, a man she had hated, but who was beginning to get beneath her skin as no one else ever had.

She would not go so far as to say it was love. There could never be anything like that between them. That would be far too dangerous a trap to fall into. Mitchell would have her in the palm of his hand.

He was only a few minutes and then, reluctantly, she heaved herself up and took her shower, pulling on the cotton shirt again before joining Mitchell in the

living-room. He had switched on the radio and was
listening, eyes closed, to some classical music. He
glanced at her, patted the cushion beside him and
continued to listen until the piece had finished.

'Wagner is one of my favourite composers,' he said.
'How about you—what sort of music do you like?'

They spent the next hour discussing likes and
dislikes, and Justine discovered they had a surprising
lot in common. Despite her good intentions, she let
her guard slip when Mitchell's arm slid about her
shoulders.

Her awareness of him increased by the second, and
when a firm finger lifted her chin, her mouth was
ready for his. The sweet tenderness of his kiss sent
rivers of excitement through her veins, churning her
stomach, filling her with desire.

His very gentleness added to Justine's torment. His
mouth teased and encouraged her. He feathered her
whole face with kisses, nibbling her ears, exploring
their intricate curves with his tongue. Her head sank
back and he turned his attention to her throat, moving
lower and lower, expertly flicking open the buttons of
her shirt before she was aware of it. His hands and
mouth assaulted her with mind-shattering expertise,
until she felt as though her very bones were melting.

Unable to help herself, she clung to him, never
wanting to let him go, murmuring his name over and
over again, arching her body ever closer.

'I think that's enough—for now,' whispered
Mitchell, gently putting her from him.

Pain clouded her eyes, and she frowned. 'No, please,
no. I——'

But he placed a finger to her mouth, moving his
head slowly from side to side, a smile on his lips which
were still soft from her kisses. 'Too much of a good
thing is bad for you. We have plenty of time. I suggest
we pop to the shops before they close, and then we can

spend the rest of the weekend doing whatever you wish. In bed, if you like? But I do need to eat now and then to keep my body fuelled.'

Still smiling he fastened her buttons and helped her up. Justine rocked unsteadily and he held her a second or two while she regained her equilibrium.

The trip to the shops took no more than a quarter of an hour, but it was sufficiently long for Justine to recover, and she gave herself a mental berating for being all kinds of a fool.

Mitchell took over in the kitchen, planning to microwave the chicken to go with the remains of their picnic salad. 'You go and get changed,' he said. 'Choose something to please me. If I know Pru, you'll have quite a choice.'

Justine was not so sure about pleasing Mitchell. She did not want to encourage him again, having made up her mind that there would be no recurrence of their earlier passion. It had been a mistake of the worst kind.

But a survey of the unknown Pru's wardrobe revealed nothing very modest, everything designed to show off an allover tan. In the end, Justine selected a white dress with a full skirt and a peasant-style top which could be worn off the shoulders or more demurely on them.

Justine chose to wear it this way, brushing her hair until it shone, scorning makeup because her face still glowed from the aftermath of their kissing, her eyes a brilliant blue, her lips soft and pink. She looked like a girl in love, she decided, much to her disgust, and hoped Mitchell wouldn't reach the same conclusion. He excited her physically, but that was all.

She opened the kitchen door and smiled self-consciously, feeling strange in someone else's dress, but he did not return her smile. Instead he stared at her as though she were a ghost.

Justine moistened her lips nervously. 'What's wrong?'

His nostrils flared as he continued to stare, his eyes assuming the glacial coldness and hardness of ice.

Justine shivered. The temporary truce was over. Though why he had chosen this moment, after what had happened, she could not imagine.

'Stay there! Don't move!' The commands were shot like bullets from a gun.

He disappeared, returning a few seconds later with his wallet, extracting a photograph which he pushed beneath her nose. 'Look at that. You've just reminded me of my purpose for getting to know you.'

It was a picture of her mother—in an almost identical dress. A photograph that must have been taken when Delphine was the same age as Justine was now. In fact, it could be herself. The likeness was even more pronounced than in the framed portrait she kept in her flat.

'The fun's over,' he snarled. 'Get ready, we're going home. If we stay here a moment longer, I won't vouch for your safety.'

CHAPTER FIVE

JUSTINE should have been thankful for her reprieve, but instead she felt sad that their weekend had come to an abrupt halt. While aware that sooner or later Mitchell would revert to the antagonist he had been when they first met, she had begun to enjoy herself. He might be after her blood, but he was irresistible. The more time she spent with him, the clearer this became.

'Aren't you being melodramatic?' Justine eyed him boldly, trying to will him to change his mind, quite sure he wouldn't cause her any physical harm.

'I don't think so, not the way I feel at this moment.'

He certainly looked mighty hostile, but she swallowed her doubts and tried again. 'Mitchell, can't you forget Delphine? I'll change the dress if it will help. Despite my earlier fears I was happy in your company—and if I'm not mistaken, you were actually beginning to like me!'

'Against my better judgment! It's ridiculous the way you go to a man's head. You're lethal, do you know that? You should never be let loose. No one's safe when you're around. In that respect you and Delphine are identical. My father couldn't resist her—and although I hate to admit it, I'm beginning to feel the same about you.'

'Is that such a bad thing?' she asked quietly. 'You have my word that I've never chased a man in my life. I've inherited none of the traits you so determinedly pin on my mother.'

He snorted angrily. 'Your mother's shortcomings were not immediately apparent. She and my father were friends for almost a year before he discovered her true character.'

'And you've carried her photograph around for twenty-four years, determined to wreak vengeance? Does your father know?'

'Of course not, and I haven't carried her photo around all this time. You're forgetting I was only twelve when the incident happened.'

'So how come you have it now?' asked Justine scathingly. 'To remind you of how alike we are?' This was sheer obstinacy. He was determined to believe the worst of Delphine—and nothing she said would change his mind.

He threw her a cutting glance. 'When my father had his stroke, I removed and burnt everything belonging to Delphine—or so I thought. I'd never liked her. Compared to my mother, she was shallow, hadn't an ounce of real warmth in her, and she certainly never had any time for me. I remember her asking my father why he didn't send me to boarding school. That was when I really began to hate her. I dreaded the thought of her becoming my stepmother.'

The bitterness in his tone made Justine wince, and she looked at him coldly. 'Hasn't it ever occurred to you that children sometimes get the wrong impression?

'If only I'd been a man when it happened,' continued Mitchell, as though she had not spoken. 'My feelings lessened in time. In fact, I rarely thought about her until she died—and then I caught my father poring over her picture in the newspaper. Gerald Jamieson had everyone's sympathy. How well her secret was kept!'

'There was no secret,' cried Justine vehemently.

'My father had another heart attack the same day. Quite a coincidence, don't you think?' The hardening of his eyes made Justine shiver. 'He claimed it was nothing to do with Delphine, but I found this photograph tucked inside a book he'd been reading. Lord knows where he'd kept it hidden. I swore then that I'd find Delphine's daughter and make her pay instead.'

'And just how did you find me?' she demanded, eyes bright, heart throbbing with anger.

He looked at her mockingly. 'Fate played right into my hands. I heard through the trade that there was a bright young designer called Justine Jamieson working for Dean & Grace. I felt sure there couldn't be two Justine Jamiesons. You had to be the girl I was after. I made some enquiries, and I was right. The rest, my dear Justine, was easy. Mr Smart believed every word I said.'

'You still have no proof that my mother was as bad as you paint her,' she returned savagely.

'Oh, I think I have. I happened to meet your dear stepfather and he confirmed the whole sorry story.'

'Why would he discuss his private life with you?' she demanded. A top criminal lawyer, Gerald Jamieson was well known in the City, and there was never a hint of scandal connected with his name.

Mitchell's sinister smile sent cold shivers down her spine. He sat down, leaning forward to peer intently into her eyes. 'When I told him I knew his daughter was not his own flesh and blood—and when we discovered a mutual grudge—he let it all out. In fact, I think it was a relief to him.'

Justine closed her eyes, a faint niggling doubt beginning to make itself felt. Was there a shred of truth in what he said? Had her mother really been unfaithful to Gerald? She had certainly been away from home a lot, but Gerald had never complained. He was twenty years his wife's senior and not keen on her friends' lively parties, but never seemed to object to Delphine's enjoying herself.

She dismissed her traitorous thoughts and concentrated on Gerald's attitude to herself. 'I'm sure I never did anything to make him feel hostile.'

'You didn't have to,' said Mitchell. 'He married Delphine hoping her baby would be a boy. When you weren't, he wanted nothing to do with you. He was after a son and heir. He's such an ugly old devil, no one else would have him. He couldn't believe his luck when Delphine made her first advances. When Stewart was born he was delirious, though by this time Delphine was up to her old tricks. He turned a blind eye and let her get on with it, grateful for the few crumbs she threw him.'

It all sounded convincing, but she was not sure how much of it was fact and how much Mitchell had thrown in for her benefit. But the seeds of doubt were sown, and there was a frown on her face as she digested the information.

Mitchell swung away savagely. 'I can see you still don't believe me. Go and get changed while I clean up.'

The return journey to London was a silent nightmare. He drove like a man possessed, lips grim, face pale, and Justine sat there turning over and over in her mind all that he had told her. It sounded like a fantasy. Surely Delphine had never behaved in the manner he described? Surely her only indiscretion had been when Justine herself was conceived?

How would she ever find out the real truth now that her mother was dead? Mitchell had it firmly fixed in his mind that she must pay for what he claimed Delphine had done to his father. He would make her life hell. The only solution was to move right away from London, the further the better.

But he would follow. He would make sure she never escaped. She could foresee a lifetime's unhappiness, with Mitchell pursuing her at every turn.

He dropped her outside the flat, roaring away almost before she closed the door. Not one word had been spoken.

Justine let herself in and put on the kettle. A strong cup of coffee was what she needed right now. It was difficult to believe that she'd been away for less than eight hours. So much had happened.

No sooner had she settled with her drink than the telephone rang. Justine mentally crossed her fingers that it wasn't Mitchell intent on harassing her further.

'Justine, at last! I've had a terrible job tracing you. Why didn't you let me know you'd moved?'

Her brother's cheerful voice brought a smile to Justine's face. 'I've only been here a week. I've hardly had time.'

'You've changed your job as well. What's going on?'

She toyed with the idea of telling him the whole sorry story, but knew it would get back to Gerald. Father and son were very close, and she didn't want the older man gloating over her misfortune. It would make his day.

'I was in a rut. Warrender's is such a big company, there's more scope.' She felt that under the circumstances a white lie was permissible.

There was a slight pause at the other end, then, 'Has this anything to do with Mitchell Warrender coming to see my father?' Stewart asked.

'You know about that?' Her heart sank, though she should have foreseen it. Gerald told his son everything. They had no secrets. He was looking forward to the day when Stewart was as big a name in the law courts as he himself.

'Yes, but Father said it was something to do with the fact that Mr Warrender senior once knew my mother. But if it's got you a better job, then it's all to the good. How about inviting me over for lunch tomorrow and you can tell me about it?'

'I'd love to,' said Justine, 'but I've been out with a—friend for the day, and done no shopping. I haven't a thing in.'

'No problem,' returned Stewart at once. 'We'll eat out. I've found this superb place where they do the best steak you've ever tasted. I'll pick you up at twelve-thirty.'

It would be nice seeing Stewart again, thought Justine as she replaced the receiver. It had been a long time since their last get-together.

She wondered how much Gerald had told him about Mitchell's visit. He had not seemed unduly concerned, so she guessed not a lot.

Stewart had been equally shocked when they discovered she was only his half-sister, but he did not attribute Gerald's attitude to this, declaring she was being too sensitive. He hadn't blamed her, though, when she left after their mother died.

Justine did not expect to sleep that night, but her day in the open air must have done her good despite its unhappy conclusion, and the moment her head touched the pillow she slept soundly.

Sunday was a much nicer day than she had envisaged, thanks to Stewart. He arrived punctually and held her in a bear-like hug. 'It's good to see you again, Sis, but what have you been doing to yourself? You've lost weight, and you look as though you could do with a week's sleep.'

Justine shrugged. 'It's all the trauma of moving, I expect.' No way would she tell him that she had been forced to half-starve because of an acute shortage of money.

'But you've settled down now?' Stewart's normally cheerful face was serious.

'Of course,' she smiled. 'I'm fine. Don't worry about me.'

'But I do. You're the only sister I've got and

someone has to look after you—despite your brave show of independence.'

Stewart was tall, fair and always full of fun. There was no resemblance between brother and sister at all. He did not even look like his father. Gerald was of medium height, with nondescript brown hair and a face like an amiable monkey.

He had terrified Justine when she was small, especially as he had a deep gruff voice to go with his unfortunate appearance. But he did not frighten her now. If necessary, she could stick up for herself. She just hoped she never saw him again.

Stewart's car was a screaming yellow sports monster, and Justine climbed into it with misgivings. He grinned and fastened his seat-belt. 'A real beauty, isn't she? A present from Father for my birthday.'

'Oh, Lord, I've missed it,' said Justine at once. 'So much has happened, I never gave it a thought. Why didn't you remind me?'

'Think I haven't tried?' he scoffed. 'I began to think you'd disappeared off the face of the earth. But now I've tracked you down, I intend keeping in touch. You're worrying me. There's something wrong, I can tell.'

'You're imagining it,' tossed Justine lightly. 'Why should there be anything wrong?' She needed to pick the right moment to tell him about Mitchell's theories regarding their mother. She didn't want to spoil the day before it began. He would be as up in arms as she had been. All she wished was that her faint fears that there might be a grain of truth in Mitchell's story would go away.

'You tell me,' he said, braking violently to avoid a dog who'd decided it was the right moment to cross the road.

'There's nothing wrong,' she insisted.

'Then why have you moved into that dump?' he

questioned sharply. 'It's not a patch on your other flat. Have you money problems?'

He was too perceptive by far, but then he always had been. They had grown up very close, Stewart always trying to be the buffer between her and Gerald. Not that it had often worked.

From the moment he was born, Stewart had been the apple of his father's eye. Even at a tender age, Justine had been quick to notice this, and had withdrawn more and more from Gerald as the years passed.

On occasions when her mother was out of town, Gerald had reduced her to tears more than once by his brutal rejection. None of it had added up until the day he told her he was not her natural father.

'I did have,' she admitted, 'but I'm managing now.'

His eyes narrowed, his face for once serious. 'Not very well, by the look of it. Did you really not have time to shop, or couldn't you afford any food? What would you have done if I hadn't phoned? Justine, you must tell me what's wrong. Not now, we'll eat first. Then we'll find somewhere quiet and you can tell me properly.'

Justine smiled weakly and hung on to her seat for dear life. Stewart drove through the streets of London as though he was on the Monte Carlo rally.

Two hours later, having eaten more food in one meal than she could ever remember, they were sitting in his car on Hampstead Heath, the engine silent, broad stretches of grass and gorse spreading out all around them.

Not far away was Keats House, where the poet was reputed to have written his *Ode to a Nightingale*. The heath was a favourite retreat of Londoners, only four miles from the city centre, but it was a long time since Justine had been here.

Stewart half-turned in his seat towards her, waiting for an answer to his question.

But how did she tell him that she was being persecuted by Mitchell Warrender? That it was his beloved father who had told the man where to find her? It was such an unbelievable story, he would say she must have got it wrong.

'I didn't actually leave Dean & Grace of my own accord,' she admitted at length. 'I was asked to go.'

And at Stewart's swiftly indrawn breath, she continued, 'After Mother died and I found out about my—er, parentage, I couldn't concentrate. I'm afraid my work suffered, and as a result they got rid of me.'

'But that's unfair,' he protested. 'There were extenuating circumstances. They should have given you a chance.'

Justine shrugged. 'I couldn't make them keep me on. Besides,' she added, with a determined smile on her face, 'I soon found another job.'

'At a lower salary by the look of it,' stormed Stewart. 'I suppose they wouldn't give you a reference? I wish you'd told me; I'd have soon put them right. And I'm sure Father would have put in a good word. He knows what a good designer you are. But you'll soon prove that you're an asset to your new company,' he finished cheerfully.

And pigs might fly, thought Justine, not realising that her scepticism showed on her face.

'You don't think so?' He frowned. 'What sort of a man is Mitchell Warrender?'

'Physically?' asked Justine, deliberately mis-understanding.

'No,' he said crossly. 'I don't give a fig what he looks like. Is he giving you a fair trial? Is there a possibility of promotion? That sort of thing.'

'Not a cat in hell's chance,' said Justine before she could stop herself.

Stewart frowned.

'He hates my guts,' she admitted quietly.

His frown deepened. 'Why? What have you done?'

'Nothing,' said Justine sadly. 'It's what Mother did—or, more to the point, what he believes about her.'

'Mother?' Stewart's mouth fell open. 'What has she got to do with it?'

'It goes back a long way,' sighed Justine, 'and it's all to do with the fact that she was expecting me when she married Gerald.'

Stewart shook his head. 'So? We know about that. What are you trying to say?'

Justine heaved a sigh and proceeded to relate the events as Mitchell had described them.

Her brother remained silent until she had finished, although the conflicting emotions crossing his face told her well enough what he was thinking.

'That's slander,' he grated. 'I'll take him to court. I'll have him strung up. If I can't fight him, no one can. He can't say things like that about our mother and get away with it. Why did you let him?'

'You think I haven't tried to defend her?' she cried. 'I've called him a liar until I'm black in the face. He's dead set on taking it out on me. I don't know what I'm going to do.' A tremor shook her voice. 'I've never felt so helpless and threatened.'

'I'm going to see him.' Stewart's face was grim. 'This is the most ridiculous thing I've ever heard.'

Justine slowly shook her head. 'It won't do any good. You might as well save your breath.'

'I can't sit back and do nothing,' he said strongly. 'Delphine was my mother too. Let him try to persecute *me*. Heavens, I can see the change in you now. Think what you'll be like in a few months' time. What's his idea? To kill you off?'

'I don't know what's in his mind,' she said tiredly, 'all I know is that it won't help if you interfere. In fact, it might make things worse.'

'How can it?' he snapped. 'The man's insane. I'll have him certified.'

Justine heaved a sigh. 'Mitchell's a powerful man in the business world. No one would ever believe your word, or mine, against his. I have to put up with it. I did actually think he was beginning to like me yesterday, but——'

'You went out with him?' interrupted Stewart incredulously. 'What an idiot you are.'

'He gave me no choice,' she admitted shamefacedly.

'And what happened?'

'We went to his friend's bungalow, near Brighton. We swam and had a picnic, and it was all a lot of fun—until——'

'He made a pass at you?' growled Stewart. 'Wait till I get my hands on him.'

Justine shook her head. 'It was nothing like that.' Best not to admit she found Mitchell attractive despite his threats. 'I spilt some coffee down my jumper and had to change into something of Pru's—that's the girl who owns the bungalow. Unfortunately, it closely resembled a dress Mother wore in a photograph he'd got. The whole sordid affair came back to life. He went berserk, and brought me straight home.'

'He didn't hurt you?' asked Stewart tightly.

She shook her head.

'Lucky for him,' he grated, and then, after a moment's pause, 'I can't believe that Mother tried to palm you off on Mr Warrender senior as his baby. Mitchell's making it up—he must be—though what he hopes to gain, except the enjoyment of harassing you, I don't know. At least she was honest with Father.'

'Apparently Gerald desperately wanted a son and heir,' said Justine. 'That was his main reason for marrying her.'

'I think he did love her,' pointed out Stewart quietly, 'and I'm convinced he wouldn't condone her having affairs with other men. I reckon this Mitchell character has made up the tale out of spite.'

'I have a sneaking suspicion there might be an element of truth in it,' said Justine ruefully.

Stewart shook his head. 'How can you say that? It's lies, all lies.'

'I thought that at first,' confessed Justine, 'but he's so insistent I'm beginning to wonder.'

'I bet he is,' snarled Stewart. 'He probably didn't like the thought of his father taking up with a glamour girl like Delphine—and now he intends taking out his spite on you. The man's insane.'

'I'll weather the storm,' she shrugged. 'I think I know a way of getting through to Mitchell Warrender.'

There was something in her tone that made him look at her sharply. 'By using your sex appeal? Don't risk it, Justine. You could end up broken-hearted. His type take what they want and have no compunction about what they leave behind. In your case it will be a pile of bones, the way you're going.'

Justine grimaced. 'I can't think of anything else.'

He was silent for a moment, and Justine watched a couple of sparrows squabbling. Then he said, 'I think I might have the solution.'

Her eyes widened and she smiled, her whole attention back on her brother. 'You're a genius.'

'It's simple, really. Go and see his father. He'll tell you the truth about Mother, and then we'll know what we're up against.'

Justine's face brightened. 'Of course, why didn't I think of that? I don't like to think she was scheming and mercenary—and yet Mitchell's so convincing.' And then, on a less optimistic note, 'On second thought, no. Seeing me might prove fatal. According to Mitchell, I'm the living image of Mother. It could bring on another heart attack if I suddenly walked into his life. I should hate to have that on my conscience.'

'Then send him a letter,' Stewart said. 'Tell him you've just found out about his friendship with your mother, and that you'd like to see him. Warn him you look like her. Treat it all very casually. You never know, it might work.'

Justine was delighted, flinging her arms about Stewart and kissing him warmly, much to his embarrassment. 'I'll do it, I'll do it. Take me home, and I'll write the letter straight away.'

Stewart laughed at her enthusiasm, but did as she asked. She invited him in but he refused, saying he had to get ready for a date that same evening.

'Anyone special?' she asked archly, knowing full well that every girl was special for a time to her good-looking brother.

'I think this might be the one,' he said proudly. 'I was going to tell you about her. Next time maybe, huh? Keep in touch, let me know as soon as you hear anything from old Mr Warrender. And if you need anyone to stick a fist under his son's jaw, I'm your man.'

He gave her a playful tap on the bottom, and the next second a yellow streak disappeared down the road.

Justine was still smiling when she entered the flat, but it faded when she discovered Mitchell Warrender making himself very much at home.

'What are you doing here?' she demanded. 'You might own the place, but I'm the tenant. I have every right to privacy.'

He held out his hand, palm upwards. 'These are yours, I believe?'

Justine looked at the gold earrings she had taken off before going swimming. They had belonged to her mother and were quite valuable.

'You picked them up yesterday? Why didn't you give them to me then?' She eyed him aggressively as she took them, noting the smart navy pinstriped suit, the white shirt and spotted tie. He looked as though he'd been somewhere special.

'That would have given me no excuse for seeing you today. Where have you been? I've waited hours.'

Justine tossed her head. 'It's no concern of yours.'

'Was that your boyfriend?'

So he had seen Stewart drop her off. 'I don't have to tell you anything.'

He looked amazingly grim all of a sudden. 'I didn't realise there was any man in your life at the moment.'

'Then it's clear you don't know everything about me,' she shot angrily, 'Though I've no doubt you'd like to.'

'I intend to,' he said threateningly. 'I had planned to take you out to lunch today. I remembered you'd had no time to shop.'

'How gallant,' said Justine scathingly. 'What made you so sure I'd come, after the way you treated me yesterday?'

A muscle jerked spasmodically in his jaw as he eyed her. 'I'm quite sure you realise that I meant every word I said, but contrary to what you might think, I do have a heart. Since it was my fault you'd bought no food, I felt the least I could do was rectify the matter.'

Justine felt a small glow of triumph. Was he actually beginning to feel something for her? Was his conscience starting to bother him? But no, this could never be. He had his reasons for doing what he did, but they certainly weren't because of any softening in his heart.

She looked at him steadily. 'I'm sorry I was out.'

He snorted savagely. 'No, you're not. You've been out with some maniac in that yellow peril. It's a wonder he didn't get you killed.'

She smiled sweetly. 'It might have been the perfect solution—to both our problems.' Now that she had decided to write to his father, she was no longer afraid of him. In fact, as the minutes ticked by she felt once again those quickened heartbeats that were a signal of her awareness.

It was insanity, really, and she was glad she hadn't told Stewart how deeply her feelings for Mitchell Warrender ran. He would have called her all sorts of an idiot—which she supposed she was—but she could do nothing about her emotions. They happened whether she liked it or not.

A sudden hideous thought that she could be falling in love ran through her mind. For a second she stood there appalled, her face mirroring her thoughts. Then she turned and held open the door. 'If you wouldn't mind leaving? I have things to do.'

'What a busy life you lead,' he sneered. 'I see no rush. Why don't you offer me a cup of coffee?'

'Because I jolly well don't want to,' shot Justine angrily. 'If you didn't help yourself, then that's your hard luck.'

'Would I do that, in someone else's flat?' he enquired blandly.

Justine shook her head in exasperation. 'You let yourself in. If that wasn't taking a liberty, I don't know what is.'

The more they crossed swords, the more aware she became of him, her whole body responding in a manner that was alien. What was it about this man that drew her to him as surely as a moth to a flame—with an equally determined fate? She wished she knew. But no matter what her feelings were, she still intended writing to his father. She would not let Mitchell continue intimidating her. It was inhuman.

She wished she could think of him as inhuman all the time, but sadly this was not the case. When he kissed her, it was as though she was the only girl in the world who had ever meant anything to him. She soared to the heights and was prepared to let him do what he liked. It was always he who called a halt.

Perhaps this should tell her something? It certainly proved what a strong will he had, far stronger than her own.

'So I'm not invited to stay any longer?'

The disappointment on his face looked genuine, and Justine felt a pang of conscience. But she quickly told herself that she was being stupid, and shook her head.

He lifted his broad shoulders in an expressive shrug and came towards her. Justine still held the door. She had been clinging to it like a lifeline; now she let it go and moved.

But not far enough. He stopped at her side, compelling her to look at him. The magnetism in his eyes had never been so strong. Justine was transfixed by it, electric impulses shooting through her, making her writhe in a silent agony of longing.

She became aware of her body leaning slowly towards him, heat enveloping her, setting her on fire; then, with an angry, self-deprecating cry she swung away.

He laughed harshly and left, swinging the door behind him so that it closed with a resounding bang. Justine felt totally humiliated.

He knew exactly the sensations that raged through her like a boiling lava stream. He was aware of his power over her—and would not hesitate to use it to his advantage.

Without more ado, Justine sat down and penned her letter. If he hadn't crowed with triumph, she might have changed her mind. He was a Jekyll and Hyde character. She never knew from one moment to the next what sort of mood he would be in. Tantalising, teasing, tormenting—they were all tricks he unashamedly used—and she almost fell for them every time.

On her way to work the next morning, Justine posted her letter, and over the next few days she waited in a state of suspense for a reply.

Stewart phoned constantly to make sure she was coping, and she was happy to relate that Mitchell was out of the office more than he was in, so that she rarely saw him.

Desmond Hunt continued to be well pleased with her work and said that he intended putting in a glowing report.

Justine let him get on with it. She knew exactly the sort of reception that would get, but there was no point in arousing Desmond's suspicions by telling him not to bother. He had no idea of the private war between her and their boss.

On Friday she received the awaited letter, and in an agony of suspense tore open the envelope, sliding out the single sheet of paper. James Warrender had been surprised but pleased to hear from Delphine's daughter, and would be delighted to see her at any time.

Justine felt elated. The note was brief, the spidery writing telling her he had difficulty in holding a pen, but she gained the impression that he was a gentle, kindly old man, nothing at all like his domineering son.

The problem now was choosing a time for her visit. If she ran into Mitchell, he would throw her out before she even got the chance to see his father.

The weekend, therefore, was unthinkable. Tonight, perhaps? The sooner the better so far as she was concerned. But would Mitchell be home? There was no way of finding out. She was not friendly enough with his secretary to ask what his plans were.

Unless she went this morning, before going to work? She could phone in and say that something had cropped up and she would be late. And Mitchell would definitely not be home then because he always arrived at the office early.

Excitement ran high in her as she went over in her mind what she would say to Mr Warrender. She would have to tread carefully and not get him over-excited.

But she felt sure that a word in Mitchell's ear from his father would work wonders. Mitchell respected and loved his parent. He would not want to do anything that might upset him.

She dressed carefully in a pink suit that was very modern and could not possibly resemble anything her mother might have worn. Makeup she kept to a minimum, a dab of powder and the merest hint of lipstick. Delphine had always taken great pains with her makeup, vivid eye-shadows and thick mascara, blusher and bright lipsticks. She looked like a painted doll, Stewart had once told her. Justine wanted to avoid this image at all costs.

As she made her way to the tube station, Justine had belated misgivings as to what reprisal she might get if Mitchell found out. The whole exercise could go wrong and explode in her face. It was a thought she dared not contemplate. It would work. It had to.

Mr Warrender's house, on the edge of Regent's Park, was a picture of classical elegance. Cream stucco, stately pillars, square-paned windows blinking in the bright morning sunlight, sweeping lawns and shelter-ing shrubs.

It breathed expensive living, and it became apparent to Justine that both Mr Warrender senior and Gerald Jamieson enjoyed similar lifestyles. And, according to Mitchell, her mother had set her cap at the two of them! She prayed with all her heart that it wasn't true. Always she had found her mother sweet and loving; never, ever thinking of herself.

But that was what she was here for. Mr Warrender

would tell her the news she wanted to hear, and Stewart would make sure Mitchell got what he deserved.

She mounted the scrubbed stone steps and rang the gleaming brass bell, her heart pounding fit to burst. A tall, elderly woman with a plain yet somehow interesting face answered.

'Good morning. My name's Justine Jamieson. I'd like to see Mr Warrender, please.' Justine smiled confidently, hoping her inner apprehension did not show.

'Is he expecting you?' The woman's voice had a pleasant Scottish lilt.

'In a way,' said Justine. 'He said I could come any time. I hope it's not too early? He is up?'

'Rises with the lark,' smiled the woman. 'Step inside. I'll tell him you're here.'

Justine climbed the last two steps and discovered that the woman was not so tall as she had thought. Clearly she was the Warrenders' housekeeper, and a treasure, judging by the fresh just-polished appearance of the house.

Justine was shown into an elegant drawing-room with a soft blue carpet and silken wall hangings, priceless pieces of porcelain displayed in glass-shelved niches. Chairs upholstered in deep rose velvet invited her to relax, but Justine simply looked about her in admiration.

No expense had been spared yet it was not a showpiece. The room had a comfortable atmosphere, and Justine was entranced. She crossed to the tall windows and looked out at the park with its green avenues and attractive lake, and could understand Mr Warrender's not wanting to leave.

A sound behind made her turn and she swung around, catching her breath and giving a cry of distress when she saw Mitchell himself standing there—and he did not look at all pleased!

CHAPTER SIX

JUSTINE's mouth fell open and her heart sank. It had never occurred to her for one moment that the housekeeper would think she meant Mr Mitchell Warrender. She had not even expected him to be at home this time in the morning.

'What the hell are you doing here?' Mitchell's tone was murderous, eyes narrowed until they were no more than two menacing slits, face as hard as chiselled marble, fists clenched threateningly at his side. 'Don't you know what it will do to my father if he catches sight of you?'

His steely tone sent a warning shiver down Justine's spine, but she lifted her chin and faced him bravely. There was no point in trying to bluff her way out of the situation. She opened her bag and pulled out his father's letter. 'He wants to see me.'

It took him hardly a second to read the few lines, drawing in a swift, disbelieving breath. 'You wrote to him?'

She nodded, her blue eyes intent in his face. Now she had got this far, she had no intention of giving up.

'Why? I've told you about his condition. Your visit could kill him.'

'Has my letter done any harm?' Justine demanded swiftly. 'Has he been any worse this last week?'

She saw that he hadn't, even before Mitchell spoke. 'No, I suppose not. But you took a risk, and you're taking no more. I don't know what you're up to, but I want you out of here—now! I'll drive you to work, and on the way you can tell me exactly why you want so desperately to see my father.'

He took her arm in a forcible grip and propelled her towards the door. Justine struggled furiously. 'Let me go, you beast. Your father's agreed to see me, you can't do this.'

'Keep your voice down,' he muttered savagely.

'I'll scream if you don't take your hands off me,' she declared. 'And then your father will know I'm here, whether you like it or not.'

'He already knows.' A new voice sounded from the doorway. So intent had they been on each other, that neither had heard the approach of Mitchell's father.

Justine jerked her head and saw a white-haired gentleman leaning on a stick. His back was bowed, but it did not disguise the fact that he was tall. Perhaps a little too thin, but he had a warm, intelligent face, which at this moment showed a certain amount of curiosity.

The hand that gripped her suddenly fell away. 'Father! I'm sorry. I had no idea Justine had been making a nuisance of herself. I'm just getting rid of her.'

Mitchell looked at Justine, a warning on his face not to continue her resistance. She glanced from him to his father. 'I think it's up to Mr Warrender whether I stay?' she ventured.

She heard Mitchell draw an angry breath, but deliberately kept her eyes on his father. The older man entered the room, limping slightly, using his brass-headed stick as he lowered himself awkwardly into a chair. 'She looks a very determined young woman to me, Mitchell. I'd like her to stay.'

Justine was appalled that her mother's careless attitude might have resulted in this fine figure of a man being permanently disabled, and it was all she could do to hide her compassion. But she guessed James Warrender did not want pity, and gave him a warmly appreciative smile. 'Thank you. You're very kind.'

'The pleasure's mine.' His eyes rested on her face and Justine fancied she saw a hint of sadness. Perhaps for a lost love? She wished she had caught his expression when he first saw her, but she had been so busy fighting Mitchell that his appearance had come as a shock to both of them.

'And you, son, shouldn't you be on your way?'

Mitchell glanced hesitantly from his father to Justine, and then back again. 'I don't think I should leave you.'

Mr Warrender frowned, bushy white brows beetling over grey eyes which had faded over the years, but must once have been as steely as his son's. Despite the fact that Mitchell was adopted, there was an uncanny resemblance between the two of them.

'Any shock I might have had came when I received Justine's letter. And, as you can see, I weathered that storm admirably. Away with you, Mitchell. This young lady and I have a lot to discuss.'

Clearly unhappy about the situation, and giving her a look designed to kill, Mitchell backed out of the room.

Mr Warrender gave a bark of laughter. 'He's too protective by far. Heavens, I have no intention of leaving this world yet. Life's just getting interesting. Sit down, and I'll ask Mrs Knight to bring us some tea.'

'No thanks,' said Justine at once, 'at least not for me. I can't stay long. I have to go to work.'

'That's a pity. Why didn't you choose to come when you had more time? I've been looking forward to this meeting.'

Justine glanced down at her hands. 'It's very awkward. I planned to avoid Mitchell. It was a shock seeing him. I thought he'd have left.'

'Normally he would have done,' said his father, 'but

a phone call held him up. I wasn't aware that you two had met?'

'It's quite a story,' said Justine diffidently, 'and your son's actually the reason I'm here.'

Mr Warrender frowned. 'I don't think I understand. I imagined you wanted to talk about your mother. I'm so sorry about the accident. It was tragic that such a beautiful woman should die so young.'

'You loved her, didn't you?' Justine enquired gently.

He nodded.

Justine swallowed hard and plunged straight in. 'Mitchell said that she tried to pretend I was yours.' Now was the make-or-break time, the moment of truth. She held her breath, watching him closely, waiting for his answer.

His smile was gentle, resigned. 'Delphine did what she thought she had to do. She wanted the best for her baby. She'd had no life herself, as you must know.'

Only too clearly. Delphine had told her daughter that her own father had died in the war, and that her mother couldn't cope alone with six children; four of them had been taken into care, Delphine included. She had been shunted from foster-parent to foster-parent, feeling more and more that no one loved her.

'She was determined her child shouldn't suffer the same fate,' continued Mr Warrender. 'Obviously I didn't take all this into account at the time. It deeply hurt me that a girl I had given my love to should insult me by pretending that some other man's baby was mine. It's only over the years that I've mellowed sufficiently to understand and forgive.'

'You're very generous, Mr Warrender,' said Justine quietly, saddened that this part of the story was the truth after all. But if he could forgive Delphine, why not Mitchell? Delphine had had her reasons, and they were not entirely mercenary.

'Merely an old fool,' he smiled. 'But no more about the past. Let me look at you. Delphine's daughter. How like her you are. And she married well after all. I was pleased for her. I presume it was Mitchell who told you about me and your mother? How did you two meet?'

'He—I—er, work for him,' said Justine, 'and, Mr Warrender, he seems to think he has a right to persecute me because of what my mother did.' She had not meant to say this, but now she had met the man, she felt sure he would understand.

'Does he, by Jove?' he exclaimed quickly. 'I did wonder why he was so anxious to throw you out.'

'He was afraid the shock of you seeing me might bring on another heart attack,' admitted Justine.

'A shock, yes, but in the nicest possible sense. Perhaps if I'd seen you a few years ago, before I found it in my heart to forgive Delphine, then it might have aggravated the old ticker, but not now. I can see I shall have to speak to my son.'

'If you would,' said Justine earnestly. This would be a far better solution than Stewart intervening. 'He's made my life a misery lately.'

The old man's lips thinned. 'Mitchell can be pretty ruthless, but you mustn't take it too much to heart. He's only trying to protect me. He never liked Delphine. She reminded him too much of his mother—my sister.'

He looked sad for a moment and then continued: 'Elizabeth was a difficult child and an even more irresponsible adult. She wasn't married when she had Mitchell and frequently asked us to look after him. When Mabel and I suggested adoption, she jumped at the chance. She has a husband now, and lives in Canada, but Mitchell never mentions her. So far as he's concerned, she doesn't exist.'

'I see,' said Justine quietly. It explained the faint likeness, and also Mitchell's unreasonable behaviour.

'He was heartbroken when Mabel died, and I did my best to be both mother and father to him. Mrs Knight helped, but it wasn't the same. When I met Delphine, he would have nothing to do with her. I could understand his feelings, but tried to explain that I was still young and healthy enough to need another woman to love, and I loved Delphine. Probably for the very reason that she was so different from Mabel. No one could take Mabel's place, ever. But life had to go on.'

'And then you found that she didn't return your love, merely wanted a father for her baby—me!' said Justine sadly. 'I'm so sorry.'

'Don't be,' said Mr Warrender gently. 'Looking at you, talking to you, seeing the type of girl you are, almost makes me wish I *had* married Delphine. You're exactly the sort of girl I'd have liked for a daughter. It upset me and Mabel very much that we weren't able to have children of our own.'

There was silence for a moment, then Justine said, 'Thank you for telling me all this, Mr Warrender. It explains so much. Perhaps you ought not to say anything to Mitchell, after all? I can understand now why he feels as he does.'

'Maybe, but it doesn't excuse his behaviour,' he said sharply. 'You claim he's been persecuting you. How?'

'I'd rather not say.' Justine kept her tone quiet. 'It doesn't seem so important in the light of what I've just heard.'

'It was important enough for you to contact me. You must have known how angry Mitchell would be if he found out?' The grey eyes looked at her pensively.

Justine nodded. 'I think he's waging the war on your behalf.'

'Probably,' sighed the old man. 'He knows I forgave Delphine eventually, but he called me all kinds of a fool for it, and he won't forgive her, even though she's no longer alive. I'll have a word with him, though. He has no right to take it out on you.'

'Thank you,' smiled Justine, trying to look relieved but suddenly doubtful that whatever his father said would make any difference. 'Now I must go—or I'll get the sack.' Her attempt at humour failed to draw a response from Mr Warrender.

He looked at her, sadly shaking his head. 'You're so much like your mother. Goodbye, my dear. Forgive me if I don't see you out.'

'Goodbye, Mr Warrender.' Impulsively she pressed a kiss to his brow, wishing that Delphine had married this man. He was what a real father should be. Nothing at all like Gerald Jamieson.

'Justine!'

She had reached the door when he spoke.

'Come and see me again. It would make an old man very happy.'

It would make her happy too, but Mitchell? He would never agree to her visiting his father. 'I'd like to,' she said slowly, 'but I don't think it's advisable.'

'Mitchell's out of the country quite often,' he said astutely.

She grinned. 'So he is. In that case, I'll be delighted.'

Justine still felt extraordinarily happy when she arrived at Warrender's Shoes. James Warrender was a darling, and she loved him. It was a pity his son was such a pig.

But her euphoria did not last. No sooner had she entered her office than Desmond Hunt said Mitchell Warrender wanted to see her.

She ought to have expected it. What on earth had made her think all would be well? But she would enter into no arguments. She would suggest he contact his father before pitching into her yet again.

Her cheeks were as pink as her suit when she tapped

on his door, her heart clamouring. She wondered whether the time would ever come when she would be able to face this man without an impending sense of doom?

A pair of savage dark-grey eyes greeted her when she obeyed the command to enter. She closed the door and stood in front of it, returning his gaze with defiance. Her heart beat a drum tattoo against her breastbone.

'Well?' he said, his tone like the cutting edge of a knife, his aggression only accentuating his masculinity.

'Well, what?' demanded Justine.

'I think you owe me an explanation. You've just done an extremely stupid and dangerous thing.'

Justine's chin lifted with characteristic stubbornness. 'I wrote him a very careful letter. I made certain my appearance wouldn't be a sudden shock.'

'How could you be sure?' he demanded, eyes glittering like diamonds.

Justine hesitated. 'I suppose not one hundred percent, but I had no other choice.'

'Choice?' A frown carved twin vertical grooves in his brow. 'Exactly why did you go to see my father?'

Her blue eyes widened innocently. 'You'll find out, I'm sure, without my telling you.'

'Believe me, I will,' he said strongly. 'I'm going home now, right this minute, and if I find that——' He broke off as his phone rang, and snatched up the receiver. 'Jayne, I thought I told you not to put through——'

His face went suddenly pale as he listened, his eyes narrowing on Justine, effectively pinning her to the spot. A lump rose in her throat. 'Oh, God,' she prayed silently, 'Please don't let it be his father.'

But her prayers went unanswered. Mitchell crashed down the receiver and snatched up his jacket from the back of a chair. 'My father's in hospital, thanks to you.' Pain ravaged his face, making him ugly and fearsome. 'If anything happens to him, you'd better look out! In fact, do yourself a favour and leave now, because if you're around when I get back I won't be responsible for my actions.'

Justine was appalled. There had certainly been no sign that her visit had upset James Warrender. He had been in high spirits, in fact. Unless that was it, he'd got too excited? A lump rose in her throat, threatening to choke her. This was the one thing she had been so careful to avoid.

'Mitchell, I must come with you,' she cried. 'If it's my fault, I want to be there. Your father liked me, he really did. He asked me to go and see him again.'

'Over my dead body,' he growled. 'You and yours have caused enough unhappiness to my family. I was wrong when I thought I could wreak vengeance on you. It was a mistake to bring you into my life. I want you to get out. Leave the country. Do what the hell you like—but just make sure I don't see you again. Is that understood?'

He pushed his face up close against hers and Justine backed away. He was so angry that there was no point in arguing. She closed her eyes as a shudder passed through her. The next second, he pushed her roughly to one side and disappeared.

For an age Justine stood there, her whole world collapsing about her shoulders. She was jobless, homeless, and desperately unhappy. She had caused Mr Warrender to have another heart attack—and just made the monumental discovery that she loved his son!

It should have been accompanied by a fanfare of trumpets. She should be viewing the world through rose-coloured spectacles. Instead, she had never felt so thoroughly miserable and lonely in her life.

It was difficult to comprehend that she loved

Mitchell. From the beginning she had felt a physical awareness, but nothing more, surely? He had never treated her as anything other than an enemy. Even his lovemaking had been tempered with hatred. And yet she was devastated now that he had cut her out of his life.

The situation was insane. Mitchell had always expressed contempt for her, would never feel any differently. So why did she love him? And why had it taken such a crippling blow to make her realise it?

Justine's footsteps dragged as she made her way back to the Design Department and began gathering up her belongings. Desmond Hunt rushed up to her, looking worried. 'What's going on?'

'I've been fired,' she said quietly.

'I beg your pardon?' His frown was deep and puzzled. 'I can't believe that. What's gone wrong?'

Justine shrugged. 'I'm afraid it's personal.'

He looked at her sharply. 'You've not been making a fool of yourself over him? I know he's a ladykiller, but I thought you had more sense.'

Justine smiled ruefully. 'Nothing like that, and you wouldn't believe me if I told you. It's too ridiculous for words. I can hardly credit it myself.'

Straightening, she clutched her bag, looking round for Fran but not seeing her. 'Thank Fran for all the help she's given me, will you? She was a good friend when I needed someone.' And she needed someone now, but not Fran, not anyone connected with Warrender's Shoes. The break had to be complete.

She went back to the flat and phoned Stewart. He was out, but his secretary said she would ask him to return the call. The time went inexorably slowly as she waited.

She wondered which hospital Mr Warrender had been taken to, and wished she had asked. She would have liked to phone and find out how he was. She felt so responsible. She tried his home number, thinking Mrs Knight might be there, but got no answer. She must have gone to the hospital, too.

And then at last Stewart phoned. Justine poured out her story, and he groaned and promised to collect her. 'Lalage, that's my girlfriend,' he explained with a smile in his voice, 'will let you stay with her, I'm sure.'

Justine wished she had known about Stewart's girlfriend before; then she wouldn't have been beholden to Mitchell.

In a little over an hour he arrived, the yellow peril replaced by a sedate grey Rolls. 'Gerald insists on my creating a good impression when I'm working,' he grinned, slinging her cases unceremoniously on to the back seat.

'So my suggestion wasn't a good one, after all?' he continued, jumping in beside her. 'Still, if it's got Mitchell Warrender off your back, that's something.'

He did not look in the least dismayed, and Justine shot him an angry glance. 'Mr Warrender's in hospital, Stewart, don't be so flippant. It's all my fault. I should never have gone there.'

'It's his son who's at fault,' returned Stewart heatedly, his good humour fading abruptly at her worried tone. 'If he hadn't set out to ruin you, none of this would have happened.'

'True,' admitted Justine, 'but I can't put all the blame on him. He was only thinking of his father. And it's right about Mother, she did try to pretend I was his. Fortunately Mr Warrender's got over it now. He no longer minds.'

'So why doesn't he tell his son that?'

'Mitchell knows,' sighed Justine. 'This is his own personal vendetta. He didn't like Mother and he's not prepared to forgive her. But James Warrender's going to have a word with him, so it should be all right,' she finished with more confidence than she felt.

Stewart gave her a doubtful glance but said no more, and in less than a quarter of an hour they reached Lalage's place. She lived in a neat little terraced house in Chelsea, squashed in a row overlooking the Thames; the paintwork pristine, windows gleaming, Nottingham lace hiding the interior from inquisitive eyes.

Lalage met them at the door and Justine liked her on sight. She had startling red hair that hung straight and silken to her shoulders. She was tall and willowy with wide green eyes and a disarming smile.

'Justine, do come in. How awful to be homeless. You must stay with me for as long as you like. Stewart, darling, why didn't you tell me before that you had this charming sister?'

'Half-sister,' he corrected with an impish grin, 'and father disowned her—so I did too.'

'Liar!' returned Justine affectionately. 'Take no notice, Lalage. It's just that we temporarily lost touch.'

'Well, I'm glad you've found each other again,' said the red-head with a smile. 'Come on, I'll show you your room,' Stewart trailed behind with the luggage.

Furnished in cream, pink and green, it was a pretty, feminine room and Justine loved it, unconcerned that there was no view in this side of the house.

Lalage turned out to be an artist and showed Justine her studio attic, which, with a large skylight, received all the natural light she needed.

'I spend all my time up here,' she informed her guest, 'so you must never feel that you're intruding. I won't even be aware of your presence.'

During the next few weeks, Justine spent her time cleaning the house, cooking their meals and generally making herself useful, feeling this was the least she could do as she was only able to contribute a small amount towards the housekeeping.

Most evenings she was alone, refusing Stewart's invitation to join them at the theatre or a restaurant, or wherever they happened to be going. She felt she was intruding into their lives enough already.

She knew that soon she would have to think about moving. It was wrong to abuse Lalage's hospitality, not that the girl seemed to mind. But she could not stay here forever.

Finding another job worried her more than she cared to admit. It was impossible to carry on with her career as a shoe designer, Mitchell had made sure of that. But there must be something she could do.

Perhaps it would be best to start afresh in another part of the country? Perhaps leave England altogether? At least then there would be no chance of running into Mitchell.

He and his father were never far from her thoughts. The alarming discovery that she loved him was uppermost at all times. She tried to tell herself that he meant nothing to her, but she had only to recall her devastation when he banished her to know that her love was very, very real.

Each hour that passed she longed for him, ached to feel his body close to hers, his lips and hands creating sensations that only he could make her feel.

She worried too about his father and several times rang his house. But Mrs Knight always announced, in the same apologetic tone, that she was not at liberty to say anything.

Mitchell really did have it in for her, thought Justine, her heart so heavy these days that life was almost unbearable. If it hadn't been for Lalage's cheerfulness, and Stewart's deep concern, she did not know how she would have coped.

Justine had never been the type to feel sorry for herself, always of the opinion that life was what you made it. But her predicament now was certainly not of her own making, and she ought to hate Mitchell for what he had done to her. Instead, her love for him grew.

One day, when she struggled into the house with a load of shopping, she discovered Lalage entertaining him. She dropped her basket in shock, a packet of biscuits splitting open, apples and oranges rolling across the floor. Her heart banged, her pulses raced, and she stood open-mouthed. He was every bit as handsome as she remembered.

To hide her love-stricken eyes, she dropped to her knees, but Lalage immediately said, 'Leave them, I'll see to it. Mr Warrender wants a word with you urgently.'

He stood up, his expression changing from one of real interest in whatever he and Lalage had been discussing to total hostility. 'My father wants to see you,' he said abruptly.

'How is he?' she asked at once, forgetting her excitement. 'I tried to find out but——'

'Not well, thanks to you,' he cut in abruptly. 'Come along. I've already wasted an hour.'

The warm glow she had felt on seeing him began to fade. She'd thought at first that he'd had a change of heart. This was clearly not the case. He was here for his father's sake, no other reason. His own feelings were no different.

But she did want to see his father. Her conscience troubled her where James was concerned. She picked up her bag. 'I'm ready,' she said.

It was not until they were in the close confines of his car that her awareness began to surge to the surface again. The woody scent of his aftershave teased her nostrils, heightened her feelings, and it was all she could do to sit still.

Mitchell looked devastating in a pair of light navy

velvet trousers and an ice-blue knitted shirt which emphasised every muscle of his magnificent torso.

'I've had the devil's own job tracing you.' He threw her a barely civil glance. 'And Miss Brancombe was not very forthcoming. What are you doing there?'

Good for Lalage, thought Justine. She had told the red-head all about Mitchell's persecution, and the girl had been shocked that any man could be so ruthless.

She ignored his last question. 'It's not surprising you've had difficulty, since you were the one to throw me out. Did you expect me to give you my new address so that you could continue your tyranny?'

He drew in a swift breath. 'Don't push it, Justine. I'm in no mood.'

'Are you ever?' she demanded.

'My father may be dying,' he spat. 'And he is the only reason you're here.'

'I'm sorry,' said Justine, guilt immediately taking the place of bitterness. 'I didn't realise he was so ill. I tried to find out, but Mrs Knight would tell me nothing.'

'On my instructions,' he thrust tersely.

The burden of James Warrender's illness settled heavily on Justine's shoulders. Her mother had started off his decline, now it looked as though she would finish it. How could she face him?

'Why—why does he want to see me?' she asked faintly.

The wide shoulders shrugged. 'I'm not sure he knows what he's saying these days. He speaks about Delphine as though she's still alive, and every day he asks when you're coming to see him. Something's preying on his mind, but he won't tell me what. Exactly why did you go to see him that day?'

Justine glanced at him coldly. 'Wasn't it obvious? To see whether you were telling the truth.'

'And now you know I was?'

'Yes,' she admitted, 'but your father didn't know you were terrorising me for Delphine's sins.'

His head whipped round to face her. 'What did you expect—that he'd rap my knuckles and all would be well? My father has always known how strongly I've felt about Delphine. The past is over so far as he's concerned, but I don't forget so easily.'

Because of his mother, thought Justine sadly. Delphine had always reminded him of the woman who so casually gave him away. She could understand his feelings, even though she found it impossible to accept that taking it out on her would put things right.

He swung the car between two wrought-iron gates and they entered the grounds of a private hospital not visible from the road. In fact, it was so discreet that Justine had never seen it before.

Mitchell strode towards the red-brick building, Justine hurrying to keep up. James Warrender's room looked out on to the garden. He sat in a chair, his eyes closed, and Justine was appalled at the change in him. His skin was almost transparent, the veins on his hands standing out like thin blue tubes.

He was a ghost of the man she had visited, only a few short weeks earlier, wired up to a sophisticated machine that monitored every breath he took.

Mitchell's face softened as he looked down at his helpless parent, and Justine's guilt increased to such an extent that she could not bear to look at him. It was all her fault!

Then he opened his eyes and the first person he saw was Justine. His smile was the most wonderful thing she had ever seen. It was full of love and was for her alone. 'Delphine!' He mouthed the word with difficulty.

Mitchell's mouth firmed. 'This is Justine, Father. Delphine's daughter.'

James Warrender turned scornful eyes on his son,

the only part of him that was still vitally alive. 'Of course, and I want to speak to her—alone.'

His words were slow and indistinct and Justine's heart went out to him.

'I don't think that's wise,' said Mitchell levelly.

'I promise not to upset him,' implored Justine. 'Surely you haven't gone to all this trouble only to deny your father a few minutes alone with me?'

'Now I know the reason you went to see him, I'm not so sure it's wise,' hissed Mitchell.

'I give you my word I won't bring up the subject of your behaviour towards me,' she said quietly. 'And if your father mentions it, I'll say everything's fine now.'

'Mitchell, please go,' interrupted his father. 'I don't know why you're kicking up such a fuss.'

'Because I fear for your health,' said Mitchell, touching his father's shoulder. 'Look what happened when Justine came to see you before.'

'It wasn't her fault,' he said.

'That's your opinion,' replied Mitchell firmly, 'but I'll humour you—on this occasion.' He left, with a warning glance at Justine.

She smiled self-consciously at James Warrender, but before either could speak the Sister in charge entered, a cheerful, plump, middle-aged woman.

'So you're the girl he's been asking for every five minutes of the day? How glad I am you've been found. Perhaps now,' with a broad wink at Mr Warrender, 'we shall have some peace?'

'She's cheeky, this one,' he said, with as much of a smile as his paralysis would allow.

'And you're an old fraud,' replied Sister sharply. 'Five minutes is all I'm allowing.'

When she had gone, Justine drew up a chair to his side and slid her hand into his. 'Mr Warrender, I can't begin to say how sorry I am. I never realised that my visit would cause you to end up like this.'

Sadness filled his eyes. 'Don't blame yourself. Seeing you made me very happy. Very happy. I've thought about you a lot. There's not much an old man can do when he's in my position, apart from think. I wish more than ever that I'd married your mother.'

It took him a long time to get his words out but he was determined, and Justine was patient. 'You're an old sentimentalist,' she chided. 'You probably wouldn't have been happy. I was a terrible child.'

'I don't believe that,' he chuckled. 'But in any case, it's what you are now that matters. And all I see is a loving, caring young lady, whom I'd be proud to call my own.'

Justine leaned across and pressed a kiss to his papery cheek. 'And I wish you were my father,' she whispered shyly. Life with James Warrender would never have been unhappy, he would have treated her as though she were his own flesh and blood, not resented her as Gerald had.

'I'm glad you said that,' he said, his voice so quiet that she had to strain her ears to listen. 'Because it has a lot, in fact it has everything, to do with my asking Mitchell to bring you here. I was sorry to hear that he'd fired you.'

Justine shrugged. What was there to say?

'How far would you go to grant an old man his last wish? To make me the happiest man in the world before I die?'

She screwed up her face in agony. She hated to hear him talk like this. She didn't want him to die, not yet. It would be all her fault if he did, and she would never be able to live with herself.

'You're not going to die,' she retorted fiercely, squeezing his hand as though by so doing she could will some of her young strong life into him. 'But if there's anything I can do, then you know you have only to say the word.'

His eyes glowed with a sudden fierce intensity.
'Justine—I want you to marry my son.'

CHAPTER SEVEN

JUSTINE felt as if Mr Warrender had dropped a bomb. Whatever she expected, it was not a suggestion that she marry Mitchell. He must be out of his mind. Hadn't she made her position clear?

'Mr Warrender,' she managed at length. 'Do you know what you are asking?'

'I know,' he said simply.

'Do you realise how Mitchell feels about me?'

He inclined his head.

'Then you must know that he wouldn't marry me if I were the last woman on earth. He hates my guts.'

Mr Warrender smiled slowly. 'He thinks he does. But I know my son as well, if not better, than he knows himself.'

'So what are you suggesting?' asked Justine, her eyes narrowed, her heart thumping. The thought of marriage to Mitchell was a tantalising one. It would not only make Mr Warrender happy, it would make her happy too. But only if Mitchell loved her. In any other circumstances, it would be unbearable.

'I'm not suggesting, I'm saying quite emphatically that Mitchell loves you. Love, hate, call it by any name you like, it amounts to the same thing. He's simply a little mixed up because of his feelings regarding your mother.'

'You're mistaken!' Justine shook her head, silken hair flying wildly.

'Can you honestly say that Mitchell had never shown any warmth towards you? That he has never kissed you, wanted to make love to you?'

A hint of colour tinged Justine's cheeks at the old

man's outspokenness, but she faced him squarely. 'I can't deny that, Mr Warrender. There have been times when——'

'When you've wished for something more?' he finished shrewdly. 'I knew the day you came to see me that you weren't immune to his charms.' He shook his head and sighed. 'You young people certainly make hard work of falling in love. You do love Mitchell?'

The suddenness of this last question caught Justine off guard and she nodded shyly.

'I thought as much, so where's the problem?'

'Your son!' she stated firmly. He was one very big problem.

'I'll handle Mitchell if you promise to go through with it.'

'I can't,' said Justine, even though she wanted to more than anything in the world. It would be like signing her life away. Marriage to Mitchell would be a passage to hell.

James looked defeated, utterly weary, as though life was not worth living any more.

'Mr Warrender, I'm sorry,' she said anxiously. 'But you must realise that it wouldn't work. Mitchell doesn't love me. You're wrong there. And marriage without love would be terribly hard. I couldn't go through with it. Not even to please you. Anything else, but not that. You do understand?'

'Yes,' he said faintly. 'I suppose you're right. It was asking a lot. I just don't want to lose you now that I've found you.'

'Marrying me off to your son isn't the solution,' said Justine gently. 'Although I don't blame you for trying. But I'll come and see you as often as you like. You needn't fear that you won't see me again.' She could always time her visits so that she need not see Mitchell. He would never approve, that was for sure.

The old man closed his eyes and then, suddenly, he

looked at her, his mouth curved in the best smile he could manage. 'I have another idea. Not such a brilliant one, but a perfect solution, all the same.'

Justine eyed him warily, wondering what cunning plan he was coming up with this time. Her brother's ideas hadn't been so good, even though they'd appeared so on the surface. Why should this man's be any better?

'You can come and live with me as my companion. It will be perfect. You'll have a home for as long as you like, and I'll pay you, of course, so you won't have any money problems. How about that?'

Justine had listened in amazement to his slow, careful words. Now she shook her head in disbelief. 'Are you serious?'

'Very!' he smiled. 'What do you say?'

'It's tempting.' It would certainly solve her immediate problems. She could not live with Lalage indefinitely, especially as she contributed so little towards the household expenses. The state handout helped but was certainly not enough to pay her share.

'So you'll come? Say you will, and I'll be out of here in no time.'

'What will Mrs Knight say?' asked Justine thoughtfully. 'She runs your house beautifully. What will she think if you install another woman?'

'Mrs Knight won't mind. Good heavens, child, she'll probably be relieved. She always worries when she has to go out.'

'In that case,' smiled Justine, 'I accept. But only temporarily. I can't impose on you forever. Once I find myself a proper job, you must let me go.'

'This is a job, you silly girl,' he grumbled good-naturedly. 'I want you to stay for as long as I need you. I won't live forever—and then you'll be free to go wherever you like. And I'll see that you're well provided for. You won't have to worry about money if you fail to find employment.'

'I do love you,' said Justine, putting her arms round him and hugging him warmly.

'And I you,' he returned. 'You've made me very happy. Almost as happy as if you'd agreed to marry Mitchell. But perhaps that will come.' A sigh shook his frail body, his eyes closed, and he appeared to go to sleep, a contented smile curving his lips.

He looked so still that Justine felt sudden alarm and ran out to summon Sister. Mitchell was standing on the other side of the door, and somewhere deep down she wondered whether he had heard their conversation, but there was no time to dwell on that now.

'Your father, he—he's gone to sleep,' she said swiftly, defensively.

His eyes narrowed. 'You look panicky. SISTER!' Brushing her aside, he entered the room.

Justine was afraid to go back in. She knew how serious Mr Warrender's condition was. If he had died! It didn't bear thinking about.

Sister appeared and closed the door behind her. Justine waited in a frenzy of impatience, wanting to go inside, but not daring.

Then both Mitchell and Sister came out, the buxom woman smiling. 'He's fast asleep, and his pulse is much stronger. I think you, young lady, have done him some good.'

Mitchell did not look so pleased, glancing at her darkly. 'I'll give you a lift home.'

It was on the tip of Justine's tongue to refuse, but why should she? He had brought her here, let him take her back.

On the short journey, Justine went over and over in her mind her conversation with Mr Warrender, wondering what Mitchell's reaction would be when he learned of his father's suggestion.

He would certainly be angry, that went without saying, and would probably try to persuade his father

to change his mind. But he wouldn't say too much for
fear of upsetting him. His father's health meant more
to him than anything else.

'Why was my father so eager to see you?' The
question broke rudely into Justine's thoughts.

She glanced across, trying to hide an involuntary
smile. If only he knew! But it was not her place to tell
him. She had no desire to be present when the
inevitable explosion took place. 'He likes me,' she said
simply.

He snorted derisively. 'So it would appear. He
wasn't pleased when he found out I'd fired you.'

'So why did you tell him?'

'Because,' he said, with exaggerated patience, 'he
couldn't understand why I didn't know your where-
abouts.' He kept his eyes on the road ahead, a pulse
jerked in his jaw, and she guessed he was reliving the
moment.

She smiled. 'I shouldn't imagine your father gets
angry very often. He's a dear old man. I wish my
mother had married him.'

'Heaven forbid!' came the rude response. 'Delphine
for a stepmother? I'd have run away.'

And now his hatred for Delphine had transferred
itself to her! It was going to be difficult, living in the
same house, loving him but having to put up with his
resentment.

He dropped her off with no suggestion that she visit
his father again, no suspicion in his mind that she was
about to become a permanent member of their
household. It wouldn't be long before he found out.

During the next week Justine waited in a state of
suspense for James to contact her, but as day followed
day she began to suspect that Mitchell must have
talked his father out of the arrangement.

She told Lalage and Stewart about the old man's
suggestion. Lalage thought it hilarious, and perhaps

not a bad idea. Mitchell had not given her the impression of being the monster Justine made out.

But Stewart was firmly against it. 'It's an insane suggestion. Mr Warrender must be out of his mind. Doesn't he realise the pressure you'd be under? And you're mad to agree after all you've gone through.'

'I'm rather looking forward to it,' said Justine quietly.

He frowned and looked at her closely. 'I can't believe that. You're not thinking of forgiving Mitchell Warrender? Have you forgotten how he tried to destroy you? If you go through with this hare-brained scheme, you'll be playing right into his hands. He'll crucify you.'

He was right, of course, she knew that already, but she wanted to help Mr Warrender. That was her only reason for accepting—or so she kept telling herself. She would not admit that it was because she would see more of Mitchell and that maybe there might be a grain of truth in what his father had said. It would be wonderful if Mitchell really did love her, though she could not see that ever being true. Too much had happened for him ever to relent and forgive.

On Sunday, Stewart and Lalage went out for the day. They invited Justine to join them, but as usual she declined. 'If that man comes, tell him to get lost,' Stewart said brutally.

'I have the feeling he's talked his father out of employing me,' said Justine.

Stewart snorted. 'I wouldn't be too sure of that. It will be to his advantage.'

And he was proved right when the doorbell rang an hour or so later, and Mitchell himself stood on the step.

He eyed her shrewdly and all the old familiar sensations came flooding back. It was astonishing she could feel like this, considering the way he treated her. Why did love always strike when it was least expected?

'May I come in?'

She nodded, her heart clamouring like alarm bells as she took him into Lalage's sitting-room. In keeping with the period of the house Lalage had decorated and furnished it in Victorian style, and as she sat on an over-stuffed chair with her hands demurely in her lap Justine felt like a Victorian miss herself.

Mitchell seated himself opposite, leaning his elbow on the table with its red chenille cover. 'I expect you know why I've come?' His eyes were fixed intently on her face, as if trying to read into her mind before she spoke.

'To tell me that you've persuaded your father to change his mind?' She wondered if he could hear her heart? It sounded so loud, echoing inside her head until she felt it might burst. What a profound effect he had on her, considering their bitter relationship.

'There's no chance of that,' he said tersely. 'I've come to collect you.'

Her eyes widened. 'Your father's out of hospital?'

'This morning.'

'You could have phoned. I'm not ready. I never expected you'd agree.'

'How long will it take you?'

She shrugged. 'Not long, but I can't leave without telling Lalage. It wouldn't be fair.'

'You can leave Miss Brancombe a note,' he said dismissively. 'My father is anxious for your company.' He paused, eyeing her narrowly. 'I hope, Justine, that your presence in the house won't cause any further regression of my father's health?'

'I hope so too,' she said firmly. 'I'm very fond of Mr Warrender. I would never consciously do anything to hurt him.'

'I'm glad to hear it.' His eyes never left her face and

Justine tightened her lips. Even grim and angry, she loved him. It was a pointless, futile love and yet she had no control over it. It was like a disease with no known cure.

He looked at his watch. 'I told my father I'd be back within the hour. You'd better get packing.'

Justine pushed herself to her feet, glad to leave the room, but wondered, as she frantically crammed clothes into cases, whether Stewart wasn't right and she would be heading for disaster.

But it was Mr Warrender she had to consider, not herself or Mitchell. He would probably be away a lot of the time. Hadn't he told her that he hated London? There would be little he could do to her beneath his father's keen eye, and she would be relatively safe for the time being.

She was snapping the locks on the last case when her bedroom door was pushed rudely open. 'Are you ready?'

She glanced at him furiously. 'You have no right coming up here! What did you think, that I'd run away over the rooftops or something? I've finished and I'm ready. Let's go.' She swung a case into each hand and attempted to push past him, ignoring the swift racing of her pulses at his nearness.

But he made no move to step aside. 'I'll take those.'

'Thank you.' She dropped them, hiding a smile when one landed on his foot. 'Oh, I'm sorry,' she said sweetly. 'I didn't mean to——'

'The heck you didn't,' he growled, kicking the case to one side. 'Let's get one thing clear right here and now. I want none of this in front of my father.'

'None of what?' asked Justine, frowning.

'Aggression. You hate my guts, I know that. I've given you just reason for it. But in front of my father, we'll be friends. If you find that too difficult then I suggest you don't come. He'll be hurt, but he'll get over it.'

Hate him! If only he knew that the feeling was not mutual. But the fact of the matter was that Mitchell loved his father enough not to want to upset him, and Justine was prepared to go along with that.

When she was so long in answering, he said gruffly, 'Maybe this will help.' The next second she found herself held hard against him, his mouth seeking hers with a gentle persuasion that began to melt her bones.

Justine could not help wondering what his reaction would have been if she'd agreed with his father's proposition that she marry him. Would he have been so eager to comply then, simply for the sake of his father's health? She did not think so, even though his kiss was convincing enough.

He was certainly doing his best to make up for the way he had treated her in the past. But it wouldn't work. She knew him for the sadist he was, and even though his kisses thrilled her, sent excitement cascading through her veins, she could not allow such insanity.

With a strangled cry, she struggled free. 'That won't help at all, Mitchell. In fact, you're simply confirming my already low opinion of you. I'm sure your father doesn't wish you to welcome me quite so enthusiastically.'

'Who knows what's going through my father's mind?' he growled, his grip tightening, clearly with no intention of letting her go. 'He's really taken a fancy to you, and who can blame him?'

His fingers mingled with the silken thickness of her hair, moulding her head, imprisoning it, making sure she could not move while his lips claimed hers.

Justine forgot everything beneath the intensity of his kiss, no longer wanting to escape. Her whole body became vibrantly alive, aching with pleasure and longing, and she pressed herself closer. Why reject what she desperately wanted?

His hands once again moved over her back, holding her against the lithe firmness of his body, his kiss deepening, his tongue plundering her soft responsive mouth.

Justine moaned softly and gave herself up to the ecstasy of the moment, her own hands curving around him, feeling the sheathed muscle beneath her fingertips, wanting to tear off his shirt and rake her nails over the silken smoothness of his skin.

Her breathing was ragged and painful and she wanted this moment to go on for ever. When he pushed her from him, she gave an involuntary cry of protest.

'No more,' he said gruffly, almost angrily, and Justine winced, wishing she hadn't made it so clear she was his to do with as he liked.

'You're Delphine's daughter, through and through,' he snarled. 'How could I have forgotten? But at least now I know what to do if you should ever show signs of causing a scene in front of my father. Perhaps it won't be so bad having you in the house after all.'

Justine was incensed. 'If you think you can manhandle me whenever it takes your fancy, you'd better think again. I'll make jolly sure you never get the chance.'

His smile was slow and insulting. 'I don't think, Justine, that you'll have the strength to resist me, just as my father could not resist your mother. It's a cruel quirk of fate that has reversed the tables.'

She sniffed indelicately and tossed her head.

'I was against my father's proposition at first, very much so, but now I think it's likely to be the best thing he could have suggested. He's dealt you right into my hands.'

'You think so?' she tossed out. 'Forewarned is forearmed, so they say. I shall make very sure that you don't come within touching distance.'

He smiled grimly. 'Do you think you'll be able to stop me?'

'I shall try,' she returned—but it would be hard, very hard indeed. He had whetted her appetite, given her a taste of what he had to offer, and she wanted him with a desperation that was frightening.

A smile played on his lips as he picked up her cases and led the way out to his car. She scribbled a hurried note for Stewart and Lalage, knowing they would not be happy that she had left without saying goodbye.

'I never thought I'd see the day when I would welcome you into my father's house,' said Mitchell, as he manoeuvred his way through the busy streets. 'When I first learned of your existence, I was after blood.'

'And you're not now?' scoffed Justine. 'Believe me, I know this is going to be no picnic. If I didn't have your father's well-being at heart, nothing would persuade me to come within a mile of you.'

His jaw firmed, and she felt grim pleasure that her barb had struck. She would have liked to thrust deeper, and if the opportunity presented itself, would not hesitate. As his father had said, there was a thin line between love and hate, and sometimes she still felt she hated Mitchell.

He glanced at her sceptically. 'I'd like to believe it's my father's health you're concerned about. But I have a feeling there's more to it than that.'

Justine frowned. 'What are you suggesting?' She did not like the insinuation behind his words.

'Like mother like daughter?' he thrust, eyes widened suggestively.

'And what is that supposed to mean?' Surely he wasn't implying she was after an affair with his father? That was sick. He was out of his mind even to contemplate such a thing.

'Isn't it obvious? You have your eye on my father's

money. For what other reason would you decide to live with an old man?'

The disgust in his tone made Justine shudder. Was his opinion of her really so low?

'I see you have nothing to say in your defence,' he continued viciously, 'so I can only presume I've guessed correctly. But don't bank on getting anything out of my father. I shall personally ensure he makes no changes to his will.'

'I don't want him to,' flung Justine. 'It wasn't my suggestion that I become his companion.'

'But you wasted no time in endearing yourself to him.' A muscle worked spasmodically in his jaw. 'Maybe my father couldn't see through you, but I certainly can.'

What point was there in arguing? He had made up his mind and that was that. She gripped her hands in her lap, trying to hide the hurt he had inflicted, amazed that the lovely warm feeling had dissolved so swiftly.

In a matter of minutes they reached Regent's Park and the classically elegant house that was to be her home for as long as Mr Warrender needed her.

She felt pleasure in looking at its stately façade, the cream stucco brilliant in the morning sunlight, the window panes gleaming a welcome, and suddenly she did not care what Mitchell thought about her. Time would prove him wrong, and meanwhile she would do her best to make Mr Warrender happy.

He carried her cases straight up to a sunny yellow room with a view over the lake. 'As soon as you've finished unpacking, my father wants you to join us on the terrace,' he said abruptly.

Justine turned to smile her acceptance but he had gone. With a mental shrug, she snapped open her cases and began hanging away the clothes she had packed with such misgivings. Her fears had not lessened. This was going to be a difficult time.

She had almost finished when Mrs Knight tapped on the open door and entered, smiling hesitantly. 'Miss Jamieson, I owe you an apology. I really did want to tell you how Mr Warrender was when you phoned, but I had my instructions.'

Justine grinned reassuringly. 'Don't worry. I know how Mitchell feels about me. He's not happy I'm here now, but since his father's employing me, there's nothing he can do.'

'I can't think why he doesn't like you,' said Mrs Knight.

'Have you worked for Mr Warrender long?' asked Justine.

'About ten years,' frowned the woman, wondering what this question had to do with it.

'Then you wouldn't know. It goes back before I was born. My mother was a friend of Mr Warrender's and Mitchell didn't like her, so consequently he doesn't like me.'

'But that's crazy,' protested the housekeeper.

Justine shrugged. 'That's Mitchell. But I hope I shan't have much to do with him. I understand he's out of the country a lot?'

'Indeed he is,' confirmed Mrs Knight. 'Though he's spent longer here lately than I can ever remember.'

Justine wondered what the housekeeper would say if she found out that it was because of her. And it looked as though the battle wasn't over. When Mr Warrender invited her to make her home with him, she had thought Mitchell would rarely be there. He had now made it clear this was unlikely to be the case. He intended carrying on his persecution tactics until he drove her out of their lives altogether.

But it was his father who counted, and Justine figuratively squared her shoulders.

'Would you mind showing me the way to the terrace? I believe Mr Warrender's waiting for me.'

It came as a shock to see the older man in his wheelchair; he still looked far too frail to have left hospital. But his crooked smile was warm when Justine joined them.

'Sit down, my dear, and welcome. I hope you're going to be very happy with us.'

'I'm sure I will be.' Justine ignored Mitchell's far from friendly face and took the cane chair next to Mr Warrender. 'It's good to see you back home.'

'I hate hospitals,' he said. 'They didn't want to let me out but I assured them I had someone to look after me, and they've arranged for a nurse to come in each day to check my blood pressure.'

'Is Doctor Reece aware that Justine has no professional qualifications?' asked Mitchell, his eyes critical as he glanced at Justine.

'She doesn't need qualifications to keep me company,' returned his father. 'What's the matter with you, Mitchell? Is it because I've given Justine a job and a home when you tried to make sure she hadn't one? At least it proves I have a heart. I'm beginning to doubt whether you have.'

His speech was still slow and slurred, but he knew what he wanted to say and made sure he said it. 'And I hope, Mitchell, that you're not going to make her life miserable?'

'As soon as I've convinced myself you're going to be all right, I'm off to Australia,' said Mitchell. 'I should have gone ten days ago. They're having problems at the Sydney factory.'

Mr Warrender looked surprised. 'Then get out there. No sense in waiting. Justine will take care of me.'

'I'll wait a day or two.' Mitchell eye's were still narrowed and assessing as they rested on Justine. 'See how she makes out.'

'You're afraid I might get too excited, trigger off another stroke?' Mr Warrender eyed his son with equal intensity. 'You're wrong there. I feel more content now than I have in a long time. This girl's going to do me a lot of good.'

Mitchell looked sceptical, and Justine was afraid he might say something to anger his father. It was a relief when he pushed himself up and strode towards the house.

'He's not happy that I've asked you here,' said Mr Warrender.

'I know,' admitted Justine.

'He's said something to you?'

'No.' She had to be careful. If his father got angry, Mitchell would blame it on her. 'But I can read between the lines. Isn't it beautiful out here?' She cast her eye down the sweep of lawn to the lake with its complement of ducks, over the weeping willows skirting the shoreline with their leafy-green crinolines, the impressive horse-chestnuts and the glowing copper beeches. 'Whoever would think we're in the heart of London?'

Mr Warrender smiled, successfully diverted. 'I could never live anywhere else. This was my first house when I got married, and I intend living out my days here.' He was silent a moment, dwelling on his lifetime in this beautiful place. Then he said, 'All this talking has made me thirsty. Will you kindly ask Mrs Knight if she'll make us a pot of tea?'

'Gladly.' Justine jumped up and went inside, calling Mrs Knight, wondering where to begin looking.

She heard a sound inside one of the rooms and pushed open the door, only to find herself face to face with Mitchell. 'I'm sorry,' she said at once, 'I'm after Mrs Knight. Do you know where she is?'

'In the kitchen, I imagine,' he growled. .

'Where's that?' There were so many doors, she did not like pushing them all open to find the one she wanted.

'At the end of the hall and down the steps.'

'Thanks.' She turned but was arrested when he called her name.

'Justine! Make sure my father doesn't become too fond of you, too reliant.' There was a warning behind his words.

'I'm here to do a job,' she said quietly, defensively. 'I shall carry it out to the best of my ability.'

'You're a shoe designer,' he said savagely. 'Don't try to fool me that this is a real job.'

Justine eyed him aggressively. 'Whose fault is it I'm here?'

'I didn't expect you to join forces with my father.'

'You didn't expect we'd ever meet. A pity you didn't think of that before you began your strong-arm tactics. I'm not the type to take things sitting down.'

'As I'm beginning to realise,' he snapped. 'But bear in mind what I say. I shouldn't like to have to throw you out.'

Her eyes widened. 'I doubt you'd have the courage to do that. Your father would be furious. It wouldn't do his health much good either.'

'I know,' he frowned. 'It's why I'm telling you now to watch what you're doing.'

'Your father's already very fond of me,' she said, feeling he was being unreasonable. 'I don't see that there's anything I can do to stop us developing a deeper relationship.'

The second the words were out, Justine knew he would misunderstand, but when he drew in a savage breath, it was too late to start again.

'You little tramp!' His lips were grim, nostrils dilated, eyes a cold, hard grey. 'If I had my way you'd be out of here now.'

'I didn't mean that as it sounded!' Justine felt worried by the depth of his anger. It would not go

unnoticed by his father, and could cause unpleasant-
ness even before her first day was over.

'No?' he sneered. 'Then what did you mean?'

'Our relationship would be no more than that
of——' She lifted her shoulders '—father and daughter.
Nothing sordid and sick, as you're suggesting.'

His eyes flicked over her damningly. 'Because my
father would never be partner to such an affair.'

'Because it's not what I'm after,' she declared.
'Heck, Mitchell, do you know what you're saying? It's
the craziest suggestion I've ever heard. Me and your
father? I can't believe that you're serious.'

'I hope I'm wrong,' he said tersely, 'for your sake.'

Justine swung away. He was not worth arguing
with.

Mrs Knight looked at her closely as she entered the
kitchen. 'Has something upset you?'

Was it so obvious? Justine smiled weakly. 'Mitchell's
just been making sure I know my place.'

'He'll get used to your being here,' said the
housekeeper sympathetically.

'Too bad if he doesn't,' returned Justine, 'because
I'm staying as long as I'm needed. Mr Warrender
would like a pot of tea, please.' She had almost
forgotten the reason she was here.

As she made her way back outside, Justine sensed
Mitchell watching her, and a cold chill stole down her
spine. He was doing all in his power to make her life
unbearable.

CHAPTER EIGHT

IN the days that followed, Justine's admiration and fondness for Mr Warrender deepened. They had a mutual respect for each other and she happily sat and read Dickens or Tolstoy out loud to him, with Bach or Schubert playing softly in the background. Their peaceful hours were spoilt only by Mitchell.

He rarely went to the office these days, but Justine dared not openly resent his presence. She did not want his father upset.

There was no denying her relief, however, when he went to Australia. She still loved him, but his treatment of her was gradually crushing these feelings. Had he been friendly, then her love would have blossomed; as things were it was slowly withering, and she guessed that one day it would die altogether. It was no fun loving a man who hated you, who insisted that you had an ulterior motive for befriending his father, and who did everything in his power to hurt you.

She had not realised how much pressure he put on her, simply by being always around when she and his father would have been content alone, his assessing grey eyes watching every move she made.

Mr Warrender did not seem to notice. In fact, he enjoyed having his son at home. Justine sometimes wondered whether it was because he still hoped she and Mitchell would fall in love. Her lips twisted wryly whenever her thoughts ran in this direction. There was no hope of that. In fact she had conditioned herself to the fact that Mitchell would never love her, and worked very hard at burying her own feelings.

But his father noticed that her smile was more ready, her eyes not so wary, once Mitchell had gone. 'Is my son still harassing you?' he enquired one day.

She shook her head. 'He rarely speaks to me, except in front of you.'

'But you're glad he's gone?'

She agreed.

'Don't you love him any more?'

Justine grimaced. 'You can't just fall out of love. It has to die a slow death.'

'But you're happier now he's no longer around.' He frowned, his straggly grey brows knitting. 'Why's that?'

'Because,' she said slowly, 'he makes me feel uncomfortable. He never felt I was right for this job, as you know.' And he thinks I'm after your money, she added silently.

'You've certainly proved Mitchell wrong in that respect,' he said, still looking anxious. 'I don't know what I'd do without you. Promise me you won't worry about him any longer?'

Justine smiled wryly. 'I'll try.' He didn't know he was asking the impossible. Although she had shown a remarkable aptitude for tending his father's needs, Mitchell was not convinced.

In health and temper, James Warrender declared that he had never felt better. His blood pressure was behaving itself and the therapy helped. He was a determined old soul and already learning to walk again, announcing frequently that he intended being around for a long time yet.

'I'm still nurturing the hope that the two of you will come to your senses,' he said quietly. 'I want to hold my own grandchild in my arms before I die. It's something I've missed out on. Mitchell was five when he came to us. There's never been a baby in this house.'

An overwhelming sadness stole over Justine. 'It won't be mine, I assure you. Please don't cherish any hopes in that direction. Mitchell will never change his mind.'

'He's thirty-six,' said James Warrender. 'What's he playing at? He ought to be married with three kids by now.'

'He's waiting for the right person, I suppose,' Justine ventured, forcing herself to smile. 'It's no good getting married until you're ready.'

'Hmpfh!' grunted the old man, looking as though he would like to say more, then abruptly changed the subject. 'How's your brother?'

Justine shrugged, 'I haven't seen him since I moved. I phoned the other day. He was a bit put out that I'd left so abruptly. Mitchell only gave me time to write a note.'

'Then invite him here,' said James Warrender at once. 'Heavens, girl, this is your home now. Ask whoever you like. I never meant you to cut yourself off from your family.'

'I have no intention of doing that,' she reassured him. 'It's just that I've been so busy.'

'Looking after a demanding old man?' he suggested ruefully.

Justine gave him a hug. 'Less of the demanding. I enjoy what I'm doing.'

'No regrets that you're not carrying on with your career?'

'What career?' she could not help asking bitterly, then smiled to soften her words. Mr Warrender could not be expected to feel the same as she did about his son.

But in that respect she was wrong. 'Mitchell will get over his animosity in time. Now you're living here, he'll soon see that you're nothing like Delphine—except in looks,' he reflected. 'She was about your age when I met her. In fact, when I first saw you it was like seeing Delphine all over again.'

'And was that what caused your heart attack?' ventured Justine faintly.

'No!' His response was emphatic. 'It was one of those inexplicable things. I was prepared for you, don't forget. You're like Delphine and yet not like her. You have a gentle caring nature, which she never had. Admittedly she put on a good act, but she was out for what she could get. She set her sights high, and although I admire ambition I cannot tolerate lies.'

'Didn't you know that she was seeing another man at the same time as you?' asked Justine gently.

He shook his head, looking sad. 'I never suspected. She really conned me. She seemed so sweet and beautiful, so very devoted. I'd never met anyone like her. I'm afraid I made a fool of myself.'

'You weren't to know,' said Justine, holding his hand, stroking the veins that stood out so prominently. His skin was almost transparent. 'And according to Mitchell, she was unfaithful to Gerald too.'

'Did he know?'

She shrugged. 'Apparently, but he turned a blind eye, so long as she was discreet. I believe he thought that better than a divorce. Actually, I still find it hard to believe. I certainly never suspected. What do you think? Do you think Delphine would do that to him?'

He held her hand tightly. 'I think it's just that Delphine never found the right man. She was more to be pitied than blamed.'

Justine nodded sadly and silently thanked him for putting it like that.

A week later, Mitchell returned and their peace was shattered. Justine would never forget his face the day he unexpectedly walked in and overheard her telling his father that she loved him.

James Warrender had once again been deploring the

fact that he and Mabel never had children. 'It was my fault entirely, but she never blamed me. It was one of those things and she accepted it. She was a fine woman and I loved her dearly. Mitchell made a tremendous difference to our lives, but I would have given anything for a child of our own.'

Justine thought she knew how he felt. More and more these days, he was opening his heart to her. He was a grand old man, so opposite to Gerald who had never had any time for her. She loved James Warrender deeply and was never afraid to tell him so.

'I feel as though I am your daughter,' she said, hugging him and pressing a kiss to his brow.

He nodded, well pleased. 'If I'd had one I'd have wanted her to be like you. I've grown very fond of you, Justine. Sometimes I wish I had married Delphine and to hell with everything—just so that I could call you mine.'

'I'm glad you didn't,' she whispered. 'You wouldn't have been happy.'

'Not as I am now,' he smiled. 'You've brought new light into my life. I love you, Justine.'

'And I love you,' she said firmly.

It was at this point that Mitchell walked in. 'What the devil's going on?'

Justine jumped at the sound of his voice, jerking her head round, her heart hammering with both excitement and dismay. She had missed him even though she had been loath to admit it, and the sight of his tanned handsome face and his perfect body set her nerve-ends tingling, even though it was clear he was not pleased to see her.

James Warrender smiled, apparently not conscious of his son's anger. 'Justine's just made me a very happy man.'

'Oh yes, and how's that?' Mitchell's eyes narrowed dangerously, and Justine thought she knew which way his thoughts ran.

'Isn't it obvious? Can't you tell?' Mr Warrender looked supremely happy.

'I hope it's not what I'm thinking?' growled Mitchell.

Before he could ruin his father's pleasure by putting into words the evil thoughts in his mind, Justine said, 'I've just told your father I'm beginning to feel like his daughter.'

'And you know how much I've always wanted one,' added Mr Warrender contentedly. 'In fact, Mitchell, I suppose I should thank you for finding her.'

'Don't bother,' he grated, turning abruptly and leaving the room.

'Looks as though he's had a hard time of it down under,' said his father. 'He'll be all right once he's had a good night's sleep.'

Justine wondered. James had no idea that his son thought they were indulging in an affair, that she was trying to trick him into marriage—as her mother had!

The thought sent icy shivers down her spine, and more than anything she would have liked to run and hide. But she had to stay with James. It was normal for them to spend their evenings together, sitting outside putting the world to rights, or, if it rained, listening to music indoors.

Within an hour Mitchell had rejoined them, showered and changed into navy velvet trousers and a white knitted shirt which complemented his wonderful tan. His hair curled crisply and he smelled of his usual spicy aftershave, but he was in no better humour.

'How're things in Sydney?' asked his father. 'Have you managed to sort them out?' He still took a keen interest in all that went on.

For the next ten minutes, they discussed the problem there, which had apparently been the result of bad design.

'Maybe,' said Mitchell slowly, a calculating eye on Justine, 'I ought to send you out there? They could do with your fresh approach.'

Sudden alarm surfaced in her. He couldn't do that to her! She wouldn't let him. But neither would his father. 'Over my dead body,' James threatened. 'She's in my employ now, and don't you forget it.'

He spoke so emphatically that Justine felt afraid. He shouldn't get worked up like this.

'It's all right, I didn't mean it.' Mitchell, too, had seen his father's distress and quickly put matters right, but Justine knew that he had been very serious, very serious indeed. It would have been the perfect solution so far as he was concerned.

He changed the subject and dismissed her by helping his father to bed himself. It was still early, so she took a walk in the park, watching the Canada geese with their long black necks, the moorhens and mallard, as well as the countless other varieties which made their home on the banks and little islands in the lake.

When a hand fell on her shoulder she jumped violently, fearing it was Mitchell. She spun on her heel, her blue eyes wide, but it was Stewart who laughed into her face. She gave a squeal of pleasure and wrapped her arms around him, accepting his big brotherly hug. 'What are you doing here?'

'Waiting for Lalage. She's gone jogging with a friend. It's her latest craze.'

'Why don't you join her?' Justine shaded her eyes against the westering sun, trying to pick out Lalage from all the other joggers who used Regent's Park as their pacing ground.

'Not likely,' he grinned. 'Come and sit down, and tell me how things are going. I saw that Mitchell Warrender guy the other day. It was all I could do to stop myself picking a fight.'

'He's been to Australia,' said Justine. 'It was very peaceful, but he got home today——'

'And already you've had enough?' Stewart frowned. 'Why don't you leave?'

She shook her head. 'I couldn't do that to his father. He's so nice, so kind and considerate. I love him.'

'With a son like Mitchell?'

She pulled a face. 'Mitchell's adopted. He's James's sister's child, actually.'

'So you've fallen for the old guy? Shame on you, Justine, I didn't think you were like that.'

She pulled a pained face. 'I don't think that's funny.'

'Heck, it was only a joke,' he said. 'What's wrong?'

'Because that's precisely what Mitchell thinks. He's convinced I've set my sights on his father so I can inherit his money.'

'Roughly what he accused Mother of. That's disgusting, if you ask me.'

'Precisely,' said Justine bitterly, 'but I have to stick it out. His father's grown really fond of me, and it would break his heart if I left. I just hope that Mitchell won't be at home often. I can put up with him for short periods.'

'I can't understand you,' said Stewart, shaking his head. 'Why stay if he's making you unhappy? Has he some hold over you?'

Justine shook her head, but there must have been a fleeting sadness in her eyes because the next second Stewart asked, 'Hey, you haven't fallen for him or anything daft like that?'

She nodded and closed her eyes. 'That's what makes it so hard.'

'You're even more of a fool than I thought.' He took her shoulders. 'Justine, you're crazy! You surely don't hope that one day he'll change his mind?'

'I know he won't,' she said quietly.

'Then why hang around?'

'Because it makes his father happy.'

He groaned. 'And to think it was my idea you went there! If I'd known what was going to happen I'd never have suggested it. Why didn't you tell me you loved Mitchell?'

'Would it have made any difference?'

'I suppose not.' He grimaced. 'I never foresaw the old man asking you to work for him. It's an odd job, being his companion. I can't really say I'm surprised at Mitchell's suspecting you.'

'Lord, don't say *you* doubt me!' cried Justine. 'If you want to find out what he's like, come and see for yourself. He's quite willing for me to invite back anyone I like.'

'I think I might take you up on that,' said Stewart. 'See for myself what this family's like.'

'Come tomorrow,' said Justine eagerly.

He shook his head. 'Lalage and I are going away for a few days, but I'll give you a ring later. I can't get over the fact that you love Mitchell. Is that the reason you took the job?'

'No!' Justine shook her head vehemently. 'It's a futile love, I know that, and I'm doing my best to forget it. I simply want to help his father. I feel I owe him that much especially as Delphine started this whole process off in the first place.'

'I don't accept that,' said Stewart strongly, his face creasing into a frown. 'Maybe the shock of her deception did cause a stroke, but he must have been prone to that sort of thing—anything else could have caused it. And he's still around all these years later, so it can't have been that bad.'

'It's because he gave up work and took things easy,' she protested. 'Didn't I prove myself how simple it was to trigger them off? I thought we were having a nice gentle chat, yet the next thing I knew he was in hospital fighting for his life. I feel obliged to help.'

'You're a fool,' he said savagely.

'I can't help it, Stewart. I wish you'd understand. Besides, Mr Warrender's a dear. He's so different from Gerald. If he had married Delphine, I'd have had a much happier life.'

'My father was jolly hard on you, I agree,' said Stewart, 'but he gave you a good education and you were doing very well for yourself until Mitchell interfered. He's the one who's caused all the trouble, not my father.'

Justine pulled a wry face and nodded. It was no use arguing with Stewart about Gerald, because he would always be on his side—and she could not blame him. Gerald was Stewart's natural father and as such treated him with the love and affection he had never shown her. She was the odd one out, the result of one of Delphine's affairs, and unfortunately had to pay for it.

A breathless Lalage suddenly dropped on to the seat beside them. Her cheeks were flushed, her eyes bright, her red hair tamed by a lilac sweatband which matched the shorts and vest that she wore.

'Hi, Justine! Lovely to see you. I thought for a moment Stewart was two-timing me. How are you doing? I'm sorry we were out when your handsome friend kidnapped you.'

She looked very happy and very much in love as she linked her arm through Stewart's, and Justine envied her. It would be heaven to have such a relationship with Mitchell.

'Pretty good,' she said, with more enthusiasm than she felt. 'Mr Warrender's got a marvellous house. I'm really very lucky.'

Lalage nodded. 'I'm glad you've got yourself sorted out. I was a bit worried about what you'd do once I

moved. We've found a gorgeous old farmhouse near
Epping Forest. You must come and see it. It has——'

Stewart tapped her hand. 'Hold your horses, Lally,
I haven't yet told Justine that we're getting married.'

Lalage rolled her eyes skywards. 'Typical! I thought
it would be the first thing you'd tell your own sister.'

'We had other things to discuss,' said Stewart
importantly, 'like Justine falling in love with Mitchell
Warrender.'

'Stewart!' hissed Justine through her teeth.

'You haven't?' Lalage looked delighted. 'How
wonderful! I knew he wasn't as black as you painted.'

'It's not mutual, he still hates me,' admitted Justine
ruefully. 'But don't let's talk about him. How about
you two getting married? I didn't know you were that
serious. I'm so pleased. Congratulations to you both.'

And what a good job she had accepted Mr
Warrender's offer, or she would once again have been
homeless.

But Lalage was like a dog worrying a bone. 'What
do you mean, he still hates you? Isn't he aware of your
feelings? He didn't strike me as being insensitive.
In fact, if I hadn't been in love with Stewart, I
think I might have fancied him myself.' She evaded
Stewart's playful slap and looked at Justine curiously.

'I'd rather not discuss it. He doesn't know how I
feel and I don't intend telling him. Too much has
happened for him to ever change his mind.'

Lalage pulled a face. 'I'm sorry. It must be awful to
be forced to live with a guy under those circumstances.
How strange he doesn't realise it. You must be a very
good actress.'

'You don't show your love when you're being
perpetually intimidated,' said Justine quietly.

'You have my sympathy,' said Lalage. 'If it were me
I think I'd let him see how I feel. He might even be

nursing a secret love for you.' She closed one eye conspiratorially. 'You never know.'

'I think not,' laughed Justine.

And when she returned to the house a short while later to meet Mitchell glowering blackly at her she knew this was so.

It had grown dark as they talked and the lamp was lit outside, casting a golden circle of light where he stood. It threw shadows across his face, highlighting the angular planes, making him look sinister and dangerous. 'Where have you been?' he asked harshly, following her indoors.

She turned with her foot on the first tread of the stairs. 'For a walk. Have you any objections?'

'My father wondered where you were. Seems he's got used to your kissing him good night.'

Justine winced at the innuendo, but tossed her head and looked at him boldly. 'You have a sick mind, Mitchell Warrender, and I'm not going to stand here arguing.'

Without more ado she carried on up the flight of stairs, her feet soundless on the thick red carpet, her hand trailing along the ornately carved balustrade.

But if it deadened her footsteps, it did the same for Mitchell, and she didn't hear him come up behind her. She gave a start of surprise when his hand came down on hers at the top of the staircase.

'My father hasn't stopped singing your praises since I got home.' His slate-grey eyes locked into hers. 'He looks as though he's on a constant high. What am I supposed to think?'

'Whatever you like,' she said coolly. 'I know the truth, and that's all that matters to me. If you want to go around assuming the worst, then that's your prerogative.'

He looked at her long and hard, his lean body thrust unnervingly close. Justine did her best to control the waves of pleasure that raced through her, but the longer he stood there, the more her awareness of him grew.

Quite unconsciously she moistened her lips with the tip of her tongue, her eyes wide and luminous. When she found herself in his arms, his mouth claiming hers, she gave a moan of sheer pleasure.

'I'll make sure,' he threatened, his voice thick, his breath hot on her cheek, his hands moulding her urgently against him, 'that you'll never want my father in preference to me.'

'I don't——'

Justine's faint protest was cut off as his mouth closed yet again on hers. She gave up and decided to enjoy this unexpected kiss, snaking her hands behind his back, uniting their bodies, oblivious to his brief surprise at her sudden capitulation.

Without warning, he swung her up into his arms and carried her through to her bedroom, depressing the handle with his elbow and kicking the door shut behind him.

He set her down inside the room and carried on his assault of her mouth as though he had never stopped, cupping her face between his hands, not imprisoning her, confident she would not try to escape.

His thumbs circled her cheeks in slow sensual movements, pulling down the corners of her mouth, kissing the soft, sensitive area inside her lips with tantalising tenderness.

Justine felt as though she was beginning to melt. Her whole body tingled with awareness, her stomach churning with excitement.

Surely the last time they had kissed it had not affected her so deeply? Today it was as if she was being touched by a live electric wire.

He progressed from her lips to the recesses of her mouth, his tongue creating exquisite torture, mingling with her own, exploring, demanding, seeking. And all the time she held on to him, her fingertips biting into his back, her very tenseness giving away her desire.

When he began to undress her there was no haste in his movements; indeed, it was Justine who was eager, helping him with buttons, wriggling in ecstasy as his lips tasted each inch of bare flesh as it was exposed.

His hands slid down the length of her body, moulding her to his hardness, his mouth moving from her throat to her shoulders, from the soft curves of her aching breasts to their sweet pink tips.

Here again his tongue circled and teased, white teeth biting—but not too hard, so that by the time he was ready to move lower Justine was moaning and straining against him.

Finally she stood naked before him and he looked at her, touching and stroking, acquainting himself with every contour of her body, almost as though he were a blind man wanting to feel her shape.

It was exquisite torture and Justine could not take her eyes off his face. She saw passion and desire, admiration and appreciation. He was merciless in his appraisal, taking so long over it that Justine finally caught hold of him and dragged his head to her breasts, holding him there, raking her fingers through the thickness of his hair, her whole body pulsing with a desire stronger than anything she had ever felt.

There would be no peace for her now. Even if he never repeated this experiment, she would have the memory. A very beautiful memory. There was no violation, she was his willing captive, greedy for every new experience at his hands.

'You're very beautiful.' His tones were gruff as he lifted glazed eyes to look at her.

Justine framed his face between her hands and kissed him, easing his shirt out of the waistband of his trousers, sliding her fingers beneath so that she could feel the hard smoothness of his naked back.

With a strangled cry he finished the job for her, snatching off the shirt and throwing it to one side. Then, with a satisfied groan, he held her close.

The sensation of his hair-roughened skin against her breasts drove Justine crazy, and she swayed erotically, luxuriating in the feel of their naked bodies together.

'Justine, you know I'm going to make love to you?'

She swallowed painfully and nodded, her eyes hypnotically drawn to his, noting the tense muscles in his jaw, wondering whether he was going to give her an option. If he was, she didn't want it. This was the moment she had dreamt about, and no matter how she might regret it later, she was not going to miss out now.

'Do you want me to?'

Again she nodded.

'Why?'

Because I love you. Are you blind? Can't you see that? How she wished she could utter these words. Instead she said, 'You've aroused me.'

'What would you do if I did back out?'

It seemed a stupid question to her. What was he trying to prove, for goodness' sake? Some man, who stopped just when the going got good! What should she say, that she'd break down and beg him? Or, good, because I wouldn't have let you anyway?

She attempted a nonchalant shrug. 'I don't know.' Her voice was a mere aching whisper, and he knew how she felt. She could see it in his face, the sudden narrowing of his eyes. He had proved his point. He had confirmed that he was more capable of arousing her than his ailing father. Or at least that was what he thought. He did not know that there had never been the need, that her feelings for the older man were purely filial.

'Then you're about to find out.' His gentleness had gone, replaced by a harshness she found difficult to accept. Yet even as he stepped áway there was something in his face that told her he was not as uncaring about what he had done as he would have her believe.

It looked as though his soul was as tortured as her own, although that was small consolation. Whatever he was feeling was of his own making; what he had done to her was deliberate.

But she could not be angry with him. He had carried out his threat, but he had shown her consideration. He had aroused in her a depth of desire that was unbelievable, and she loved him more than ever. All she was afraid of now was that she had given herself away. But his next words proved her fears unfounded.

His passion had cooled as he pulled on his shirt, and he had clearly thought about the situation. 'I might have known you'd be amenable,' he taunted her. 'You're not Delphine's daughter for nothing. Or have I said that before? If I have, I apologise, but it's true. You're ready for any man, I should have known that.'

Justine tossed her head angrily. 'For your information, there has been no man in my life for a long time—nor have I wanted one.'

But, unlike her mother, she had now found the one man who could make her truly happy.

His brows rose sceptically. 'You expect me to believe that? Much as it grieves me to admit it, you're damnably irresistible—and so easily aroused! You can't kid me that my fellow men have left you strictly alone.'

'Of course not, but I've always made my feelings clear, and they've never pestered me—as you have!' She glared ferociously at him, and he laughed.

'So why am I different? Why let me get through you defences?'

Because I love you, you idiot, her heart cried.

What she said was, 'Let's say you have a way with you.'

'Should I be flattered?' he asked smoothly, a smile struggling to escape.

His mockery irritated her. 'I doubt it. The way I see things, it's your experience that gives you the edge. But it's all right for a man, isn't it? He can play around. Suspect a girl's doing that sort of thing, though, and it's another matter. She's automatically branded.'

'I think this conversation has gone far enough,' said Mitchell tightly, a frown drawing his black brows together, giving his whole face a thunderous appearance. His mouth was a grim straight line and Justine knew she had gone beyond the limit.

But she was not finished. 'It's odd how a man backs down when the boot's on the other foot.'

With a cry of fury he grabbed her shoulders, propelling her mercilessly towards the bed. In her anger Justine had forgotten she was still naked and now felt the bruising pressure of his fingers on her flesh.

Her knees buckled as she backed into the bed and involuntarily sat down. He lifted her legs and laid her full length on the silken cover, glowering over her, and Justine knew exactly what was running through his mind.

He was not admiring her now, he was contemplating rape, for that was what it would be. She would never let him take her in anger. When he was gentle she was his, but if he attempted to touch her at this moment she would fight with every ounce of strength she had.

For a whole minute they stared at each other in total silence, Justine lost in a quagmire of fierce emotions, her body rigid, her eyes blazing in a face now devoid of colour.

If he dared to lay a finger on her she would scream,

scream so loudly that his father and Mrs Knight would both hear and come to her aid. And what would Mitchell say then? How would he get out of that?

Maybe the same thoughts were running through his mind, because the next second he spun on his heel and vanished, leaving Justine to wrap her arms about her suddenly ice-cold body.

CHAPTER NINE

JUSTINE lay quite still. Mitchell had raised her to the heights and dropped her flat, all in a matter of minutes. He had shown her how expertly he could evoke total response, and how swiftly his mood could change—wiping away those feelings as though they had never existed.

She had been a fool to let him see how easily he could excite her, and it was no wonder he thought she was like this with every guy she met. If only he knew!

It was an insane situation and she ought to have thought about this before accepting Mr Warrender's offer. All she could do now was hope Mitchell would not repeat the experiment. He had made his point. He had, in his own mind, confirmed that he was a better lover than she would ever find his father. Perhaps he would leave it at that?

But in these hopes she was mistaken. The next day Mitchell greeted her at breakfast with a smile and a kiss—and every indication that he intended continuing his game. His father was not yet up, waiting for the nurse's daily visit before joining them.

Her eyes were a startled blue as she looked at him, but she ventured a weak smile.

'Good morning, Justine. Did you sleep well?'

Did he hope she hadn't? Did he think last night's lovemaking was too disturbing for her to relax? How right he was, but she wouldn't give him the pleasure of admitting it. 'Yes, thank you,' she said demurely.

'Liar!' He studied her face and Justine felt a quiver of response.

It was impossible to erase from her mind the

memory of his touch, the contact of his firmly muscled body against her own soft skin, with no more than the hairs on his chest to separate them.

Her stomach contracted. The love she had thought under control was unleashed, and she felt sure it must shine from her eyes. It was too powerful to hide.

He stood desperately close, his now familiar male odour filling the air, drugging her senses. She felt she was drowning in eyes the colour of a summer storm. 'You hardly slept at all.'

'Maybe I was awake just a little,' she said huskily, unable to look away, wondering whether he felt the same physical awareness.

'Enough to give you shadows beneath your eyes.' He framed her face, his thumbs gentle on the softly smudged skin. 'Were they pleasurable thoughts or hostile ones that kept you from sleeping?'

Justine tingled from head to toe, restraining herself with difficulty from sliding her arms around him and exulting once again in his male strength against her. Even so her response was total. His palms against her cheeks, the light caress of his fingers, were as potent as if he were actually making love.

'Don't spoil your beautiful face by losing sleep over me,' he said softly.

'I'll try not to.' Her eyes were imprisoned by his. Even the light touch of his hands restrained her like prison bars.

'I thought maybe I'd take you out for the day, if my father doesn't object. You haven't had any time off since you came here.'

Her heart crashed within her. Did he realise what a whole day in his company would do to her? It would be heaven and hell at the same time. 'I don't need time off. It's not hard work, keeping your father company.'

'But you're on constant call, you have to fetch and carry and please his every whim.' His eyes suddenly narrowed, and Justine knew what thoughts filled his mind.

'It's still not tiring. I don't mind what I do for him.'

His lips clamped, a muscle tensed in his jaw, and Justine wished she could re-phrase her sentence.

'That is what I'm afraid of. In the short time I was away, my father has become devoted to you. Even a blind man could see that.'

Justine heaved a sigh. 'Dependent, not devoted. You're reading something into the situation which isn't there. Please accept that there is nothing in our relationship which need worry you.'

He smiled grimly. 'I intend making sure. Now, shall we eat?'

Mrs Knight had already loaded covered dishes on to a heated tray, and Mitchell ate heartily. Justine, on the other hand, ignored the crisply done bacon and succulent sausages, nibbling a piece of toast and sipping orange juice.

She glanced at Mitchell once and caught him studying her, and dared not look again. She wondered what thoughts were going through his mind? Did he really believe she would consider an affair with his father? Was that the reason he was giving her his attention now? Or was he growing attracted to her for her own sake?

This latter was the most provocative notion, setting her nerve-ends pulsing, and she refused to accept that he saw her in any other light. No man in his right mind would entertain such discreditable notions.

'I thought we might go down to Pru's beach-house again, blow the city air out of our lungs. How does that sound?'

Wonderful! Marvellous! Exhilarating! But she quelled her excitement and smiled. 'Very nice.'

His brows rose. 'You sound like a child who's been

told she's going to the museum as a special treat when she'd much prefer the zoo.'

'I feel guilty about taking a day off,' she said defensively.

'I'll have a word with my father, if that will please you, but I know he'll agree.'

Of course he would, thought Justine, he still entertained hopes that she and Mitchell would get together. James wouldn't mind if they spent every minute of every day in each other's company!

'I'm sure he will, but I'd feel better if you asked him, rather than told him. It's only fair.'

He shrugged. 'As you wish.'

They finished their meal, Mitchell restored to good humour, telling her how beautiful Sydney Harbour was. 'While I was there, Martin—that's the guy in charge of things—took me sailing. It's out of this world. The Aussies aren't boasting when they claim they have the most beautiful harbour in the world. You really should see it some day.'

'I'd like to,' said Justine politely, but knew she would never be able to afford such a holiday, not unless she managed to scramble back on her career ladder. And to do that, she would need to rid herself of the Warrender family.

They had just finished their meal when Mr Warrender wheeled himself into the room. It was not necessary these days for him to confine himself to his chair—he could manage with his sticks, albeit slowly and with much determination. But when he was in a hurry, he fell back to this mechanical aid.

'Good morning, Justine, Mitchell.' He sounded in the best of spirits, his cheeks once again a healthy pink. 'I'm glad I've caught you before you left, son. I thought of asking a few friends round to lunch, seeing that I'm so much better. I'd like you to be here.'

Mitchell frowned. 'I had made other arrangements,

Father. I'm not going to the office, I'm taking Justine out.'

'But it doesn't matter,' said Justine at once, delighted to see her employer so cheerful. Company would do him good. It sometimes depressed him that he could not do the things he wanted. His brain was as agile as ever and it was frustrating to be a prisoner within his body. But he tried hard, and Justine knew that his determination would win in the end.

Now he smiled, his shining eyes encompassing them both. Justine knew what thoughts were in his mind. 'In that case, you carry on. I'll have my luncheon party another day.'

'Why this sudden urge for a comrades' reunion?' questioned Mitchell suspiciously.

'Because I want to show Justine off.' Mr Warrender looked proud. 'Not many of my friends can claim to have so delightful a companion. You've no idea how she looks after me.'

Mitchell frowned, his brows a black jagged line. 'I can imagine.'

Justine heaved a mental sigh. Why did he always misconstrue everything his father said? Anyone would think he was jealous.

'So you two go off and enjoy yourselves,' said the older man. 'I'll be quite happy drawing up my list.'

Mitchell grunted and Justine said anxiously, 'Are you sure? I'm willing to stay and do it for you. We'll arrange the luncheon for tomorrow. It would have been a bit short notice to expect anyone to come today.'

'You're right, as usual,' he grumbled good-naturedly. 'This girl's always right, Mitchell. Goodness knows how I managed without her.'

'The same as you will when she's gone,' snarled Mitchell. 'You can't expect her to stay here for ever. She's too young to tie herself to an old man.'

Justine winced at his brutal words, expecting Mr Warrender to show hurt, but when she looked at him he was smiling. 'What's wrong, son? You sound as though it bothers you.'

'It does.' There was thunder on Mitchell's face.

'You weren't very worried about Justine when you kicked her out of a job and a home. As I understand it, you were doing your very best to destroy her.'

There was a harshness in Mr Warrender's tone which Justine had not heard before. Even that first time when she complained about Mitchell's treatment he had not been so hard, sticking up for his son by suggesting he only had his interests at heart.

Perhaps he had not entirely believed her? Now he could see for himself the way Mitchell treated her. From the moment she arrived he had been far from friendly—until last night. But his father did not know about that.

'I was,' admitted Mitchell surprisingly. 'You know how I felt about Delphine. I wanted her daughter to suffer as you did.'

The two men eyed each other, and Justine felt worried, wondering whether she ought to intervene. The doctor had said Mr Warrender was to take things easy. It wasn't good for him to get upset. Who knew what might happen?

And again she was the indirect cause. Where was it going to end? Should she leave before she destroyed the old man completely? Tears sprang to her eyes as she stepped forward and placed a hand on the older man's arm.

'Please don't argue. Mitchell and I have——' she searched for the right words, looking to him for help. His lips twitched but he let her struggle on. 'Have reached an understanding. There'll be no more friction, I promise.'

'That's right,' agreed Mitchell surprisingly. 'I've

discovered that Justine is nothing like her mother. I was wrong.' He lifted Justine's hand, holding it between his own. 'And by the end of today, I think we'll understand each other a whole lot better.'

Justine's eyes widened fractionally but she smiled, and when she looked at the older man, he was smiling too. 'You don't know how pleased I am that you've come to your senses at last. I knew from the moment I set eyes on Justine that she had inherited none of her mother's bad habits. You must have been wearing blinkers, son, if you thought they were alike.'

'Maybe,' he conceded. 'But I remember how easily you were taken in by Delphine.'

Mr Warrender shrugged. 'That's all in the past. What matters now is that you two become friends. Run along and enjoy your day, and tell me all about it when you get back.'

Justine bent and pressed a kiss to his brow. It was a habit she had grown into during the last few days, and he obviously appreciated the gesture, touching her hair and holding her close for a moment.

When she straightened Mitchell had gone, but she quelled her misgivings and ran upstairs to collect her bag. He had the car revving when she went outside, and in a matter of seconds they were on their way.

The crush of traffic tried his temper and he constantly sounded his horn. But Justine felt it was not so much the red London buses, or the distinctive black taxis, or even the cars jostling for position that angered him, but herself once again. He objected to her kissing his father!

It was a disappointing start to the day, and as they wove in and out of the endless stream of traffic she wished she had never come. When he was in this mood, he was unbearable. It was as though their intimacy of last night had never been.

And then, miraculously, he changed. The traffic

lessened as they headed towards Brighton, and he turned to her with a smile. 'My father's right, you're nothing like Delphine. I should trust you.'

'You can't help how you feel,' said Justine, a warm glow beginning to envelop her.

'I've given you a raw deal. I've a heck of a suspicious nature. Am I forgiven?'

She nodded, feeling suddenly shy. She had never seen Mitchell so humble before.

He took her hand and placed it on his thigh. Longing ran through her. She could feel the hard muscle, the taut sinews, the power, and she wondered where this day would end? Conflicting emotions raged inside her. She felt the tenseness in him, sensed his physical desire for her, and her whole body cried out in response.

Did he know how she felt? Was he aware that her feelings ran as high as his own? He must be. For once they were perfectly attuned; their minds, their bodies, their desires in complete accord.

She looked at him and her heart melted at the tender smile he gave. 'I never thought we'd be together like this.'

'Me neither,' he said. 'We seem to have wasted an awful lot of time. But the catching up should be most enjoyable.'

Shyly, Justine nodded.

'I can understand why my father fell for Delphine if she had the same irresistible quality as you. His trouble was that he didn't give himself time to get to know her before capitulating.'

'You've certainly not made the same mistake,' said Justine, her lips twisting wryly.

'I never wanted to get involved at all,' he admitted gruffly.

She wondered how deeply involved he intended getting now. Was he after a casual affair or something more serious? She dared not hope it might be the latter. But neither did she relish entering into a relationship which would come to an abrupt end once he tired of her.

An electric silence settled over them, each longing for the journey to end so that they could be in each other's arms. Words would ruin their fever-pitch emotions. Their only contact was his hand on hers as it lay on his leg. It was as though they were locked together.

Every time he changed gear she felt the tightening of muscle, his hand leaving hers momentarily but always coming back. She wanted to lift it, to raise it to her lips, to press kisses into his palm. She wanted his love. She wanted all of him.

With each mile that passed her desire grew, and the nearer they got to their destination, the stronger her heart pounded. Anticipation raged through her like a swollen mountain stream, and she was unaware that her grip on his leg had tightened until he prised her fingers away.

'What's wrong, little one?' He looked at her with a smile, his tone soft and amused. 'Are you having second thoughts?'

She pulled her hand away, rubbing it self-consciously on the side of the seat. 'No.' This was a day she had never expected, one she would mark in big red letters in her diary. 'Today Mitchell called a truce.'

Justine had really thought she would live the rest of her life without his saying a kind word to her, without ever experiencing his lovemaking again. In the early days of their acquaintance she had been given a taste of his sexuality, enough to whet her appetite and sow the seeds of love. But she had never expected he would change his attitude. Now, at long last, he was learning to trust her.

'Then why the nerves?'

'It's not nerves, Mitchell.'

It's contact with you. It's excitement. It's hope. It's love! How she wished she could put her thoughts into words. She smiled ruefully.

'I'm hungry for you. I, too, had a sleepless night, in case you're wondering. I want you, Justine, as I've never wanted any other woman in my life.'

Justine closed her eyes and sat perfectly still, scarcely even breathing. He wanted her. He desired her. But he did not love her! This was the sad part of it all.

'Justine?' He sounded just a little bit anxious. 'Have I shocked you? Didn't you guess that was why I wanted you to myself today?' And, on a quieter note, 'I thought you wanted me too?'

She let out her breath and looked at him. She had to be honest. 'I do.' Her eyes were wide limpid pools in her flushed face. She felt on fire. Every pulse was racing, her heart working overtime.

The tense lines creasing his face softened. His always sensual lips curved into a smile. He glanced across at her. 'You're very beautiful. I don't know how I've managed to resist you all this time. Here, feel my heart.' He picked up her hand and pressed it to his chest.

It thudded like a mad thing beneath her palm, his moist body heat dampening his shirt. He was as much on fire as she herself.

Justine had never been in such a volatile situation. She felt that if they were not careful the whole thing would explode in their faces; the hunger inside them fed by the deprivation of these last weeks.

It was all she could do to tear her hand away; she needed to feel him, to touch him, to maintain contact. But it was also insanity. It gave away too much of what was private inside her.

She gave a breathless sigh and leaned her head back, unable to control a smile of happiness which now seemed to be a permanent fixture on her face.

Mitchell was smiling too. Not looking at her, keeping his eyes on the road ahead, but with her in mind, aware of every movement she made; the soft flutter of her eyelashes, the frequent moistening of dry lips. They were attuned to each other's needs and thoughts, and Justine had never felt happier.

She refused to think what might lie ahead, what heartache or heartbreak. For too long she had suppressed her emotions and today she was going to give them full rein.

At last the journey ended. Mitchell stopped at the village store to purchase whatever he thought necessary. Justine did not go in with him, sitting quietly in the car, inhaling the fresh air, listening to the silence.

She had not realised until this moment how much she needed to escape from the city. Regent's Park was a surprising haven in its centre, but, even so, there were people and traffic and hustle and bustle. Here she could unwind, relax, just be herself.

Mitchell returned with loaded bags which he dumped on the back seat, and in five minutes they were inside the bungalow.

She recalled the last time they were here, when she had agreed to spend the weekend with him. What a disaster that had turned out to be! He had been unable to forget that she was Delphine's daughter, and they'd had to leave precipitately, problems unsolved. He was over his animosity now, though, and she could foresee nothing but pleasure in the day ahead.

Once the groceries were stored away, he held out his arms and she went into them readily. His eyes searched her face, observing her hunger, but at this stage he did nothing more than hold her close.

Justine knew this was where she belonged. There was a rightness about it, and she wondered whether Mitchell felt the same. Despite the fire raging inside peace stole over her, and when he led her gently through to the room with the view, and sat her down on the settee, his arm still about her shoulders, she had never been more content in her life.

He traced the delicate outline of her face, touching her eyelids, her nose, the curve of her cheek, her trembling lips. He observed the trust in her eyes, their liquid softness, and buried his face in her hair.

She felt the tremors running through him and put her hands against his chest. The echo beats of his heart were strong and vibrant. Her fingertips tingled as though she were touching a magnetic field, and she wanted him so desperately that she arched closer, sliding her arms round his back and silently offering herself to him.

'Not yet, my little one. Don't be in a hurry.'

How could he? From where did he find the strength to resist? Didn't his desires run as deep as her own?

His fingers continued their slow caress, moving to the delicate area behind her ears and down the sensitive tendons in her throat. Justine had never known such pleasure.

He laid her down on the settee, kneeling beside her, popping the buttons on her camisole top. With tenderness beyond description he stroked the soft mounds of her breasts, circling with ever-increasing pressure, finally claiming her hardened nipples, his touch stronger now, pinching, hurting, making her cry out.

He kissed her then, silencing her, increasing her pleasure. He was no longer gentle, sheer naked desire taking over. He was bruising her lips, demanding a response, and Justine held nothing back.

This was the moment she had been waiting for, the

giving from one to the other. His mouth tasted sweet and she drank hungrily of his passion, entwining his thick black hair in her fingers and holding his head close.

His eager tongue probed her ears and throat, his mouth sliding with excruciating slowness towards her throbbing breasts. The sheer raw power of him took Justine's breath away and she heard herself gasping for air, giving a cry of pure physical excitement when his mouth closed on her nipples.

While Justine ached for him to take her completely, he seemed content to continue his expert stimulation, ignoring her whispers and pleas, gaining his own pleasure from her arousal.

He whipped off his shirt and pulled her on to the softly carpeted floor. 'Kiss me,' he groaned, his face ravaged, his eyes closed, as he lay back, her willing captive.

Justine had never taken the initiative before, but such was the depth of her desire that she knew instinctively what to do. Kissing Mitchell freely, without any inhibitions, tracing her hands over his magnificent body, was like a dream come true.

She had fantasised often doing this very same thing, except that it was not the same at all. Her perception was heightened tenfold. Touching Mitchell so intimately was like adding a flame to her already ignited senses.

Quite when it happened she was not aware, but suddenly they were both naked and he was inciting her to even greater degrees of longing and wanting and needing.

When at long, long last, after what seemed like hours of physical torment, the final moment came, it was all that Justine expected and more.

He too had his share of the enjoyment, insisting that Justine pleasure him as much as he did her, and now they lay in each other's arms, sated and weak, happy and content. It was an experience Justine would never forget.

They slept, and when she awoke Justine felt cold. Mitchell breathed deeply at her side, and she half sat, looking down at him with greedy eyes. She ran her hands lightly over his hard, muscled body and felt new sensations quiver through her.

This was insanity. She wanted more from Mitchell than physical pleasure, didn't she? The thought frightened her and she sprang to her feet.

But he wasn't sleeping at all! He caught hold of her ankle and pulled her down beside him, making love to her all over again.

Later they went swimming and then sunbathed on the sand completely naked. Justine had thrown her inhibitions away the first moment he touched her. This was the man she loved, she had nothing to hide from him.

She dared not think what his feelings were, whether this was an isolated occasion, or whether it was the start of a new and wonderful relationship—culminating, she hoped, in marriage.

They cooked lunch together and ate it out on the balcony, watching the glittering waves as they nibbled chicken drumsticks, listening to mewing gulls as they drank a bottle of Chablis.

Then Mitchell insisted they go for a walk. They held hands and laughed as they raced along the shore. She squealed as he chased her through the sand dunes, then moaned with pleasure as he threw her down and began kissing her all over again.

The day exceeded her expectations. Mitchell was an expert, considerate lover, and they did not have one cross word. Nothing could have been more perfect—except, perhaps, if he had told her he loved her. This was what she wanted most of all. But if he didn't, then she would accept what he was offering for as long as it lasted.

James Warrender listened to his son's account of their lazy day with a pleased smile on his lips. Justine knew he guessed quite a lot more had happened than they were telling him. It was there on her face for all to see.

The next morning, Mitchell went to work and Stewart rang. Mr Warrender was present when Justine took the call and made signs for her to invite Stewart to join their luncheon party, where eight guests were expected.

At the last minute, Mitchell phoned to say he could not make it. Justine again took the call. 'I'm sorry, my love,' he said, his voice a low spine-tingling murmur. 'But anyway, I want to see you alone, not with all those old cronies. I don't think they'd approve if I stripped you naked and made love to you on the carpet, because that's what I feel like doing.'

Justine giggled and blushed, and James Warrender looked at her archly, correctly guessing that his son was making improper suggestions.

'Mitchell can't come,' she said when she put down the phone, but she was not disappointed. She agreed with him; they needed to be alone with their new-found desire.

'I rather expected it,' said his father, 'but it doesn't matter now your brother's coming. We still have a nice even number.'

The couples arrived, ranging in age from early fifties to late seventies.

Justine had dressed carefully to please James. A pale pink silk with a dusky sash at the hip, and pearls. It was one of her mother's dresses which she had always thought too old for her, but on this occasion was perfect. She did not want to appear too young, though nothing could disguise her inner glow. She was a picture of freshness and vitality, and Mr Warrender was proud of her.

Conversation naturally centred on people and topics which Justine knew nothing about, but she circulated and joined in where she could, conscious of the admiring glances directed her way.

Stewart was late, much to her annoyance, but he finally arrived and they sat down for lunch. Mrs Knight had done them proud: consommé with sherry, poached salmon, chocolate profiteroles, plenty of wine, coffee and liqueurs.

The guests departed happily after congratulating James Warrender on his companion, his food and his gradual return to good health. In that order. Stewart remained, at the older man's insistence.

'I told you they'd be jealous,' chortled Justine's employer once they were on their own. 'Did you see their faces? I bet they all wish they could get rid of their wives and find a young girl like you to look after them.'

Justine smiled. 'You're an old rogue, and no mistake. But a lovable one, all the same.'

Then James began talking to Stewart, asking him questions about Delphine and Gerald, and Justine was left to her thoughts, which quite naturally settled on Mitchell.

She wondered where he was now, what he was doing? Was he thinking of her? Could he concentrate or was she a distraction? Certainly he had been on *her* mind all through the day. She had talked and laughed and made all the right replies, but her thoughts had been with him.

She had forgotten to ask what time he would be home, and hoped it would not be late. She was being foolish, she knew, probably reading more into their relationship than he intended, but she could not help it.

Women usually wanted more out of a relationship than a man was prepared to give, and it would be her own fault if she was disappointed. But she would face that when the time came. Meanwhile she would take what was offered and be grateful.

Stewart and James Warrender got on so well that the older man invited him to stay for dinner as well.

Her brother looked genuinely dismayed when he shook his head. 'I'm sorry, Lalage is expecting me. But, if I may, I'll take you up on your offer some other time?'

'Any time,' said Mr Warrender warmly.

Justine accompanied her brother to the door, and he put his hands on her shoulders, holding her at arm's length.

'You seem to be doing all right for yourself here, Sis. I must admit I was worried about you, but not any more. He dotes on you, and certainly won't stand any nonsense from his son.'

Justine smiled. 'I'm getting on pretty well with Mitchell too at the moment.'

He read the pleasure in her tone and lifted his brows. 'Is that good news or bad?'

'What do you think?' she beamed, unable to contain the happiness she felt.

'Then I'm happy for you.' He pulled her to him, enclosing her in one of his bear-like hugs. Justine lifted her chin and kissed him—and Mitchell walked in.

Justine was in time to see his smile fade, replaced by an instant blaze of anger and hatred. She knew what it must look like. He had never met Stewart and had no idea that this was her brother.

Sht struggled out of Stewart's embrace. He had his back to the door and had neither heard nor seen the other man. 'Mitchell, let me introduce——'

But Mitchell didn't wait to hear. He spun on his heel and slammed the door behind him so violently that it jolted a picture from the wall, sending it crashing to the floor with a noise that brought Mrs Knight running and Mr Warrender calling from the sitting-room.

Stewart looked at Justine, startled by the whirlwind that had suddenly swept out of the doorway. 'What was that all about?'

She grimaced. 'It was Mitchell, drawing the wrong conclusions. He's like that. He always believes the worst of me.'

'That was Mitchell?' asked Mrs Knight incredulously. 'What's he playing at?'

Mr Warrender wheeled silently up behind them, looking at brother and sister still standing close. 'Showing the biggest display of jealousy I've ever seen.' And he looked so pleased that Justine began to laugh.

What an astute old man he was. And if he was right, it meant that Mitchell was after more than an affair. It meant he loved her!

'He'll be back,' assured Mr Warrender, 'when he's cooled down. He'll be ready to listen then. He has a temper, like his mother, and acts before he thinks. Don't let him spoil your day.'

'I won't,' smiled Justine, confident now in the knowledge that Mitchell loved her.

Mrs Knight had already restored the picture—fortunately with no broken glass—to its hook. Stewart left after once again thanking Mr Warrender for a lovely day, and Justine wheeled Mr Warrender back into the sitting-room.

They decided not to hold dinner for Mitchell. 'It could be midnight before he returns,' said his father.

But Justine was on edge all evening. Why hadn't he listened? Why had he rushed off like that? Surely he must have seen it was a sisterly kiss, nothing like the ones she had willingly given him?

And then came the phone call—the police asking for Mr Warrender. Justine grew cold as she stood by his side, trying to listen to the distant voice in the earpiece.

'I see—yes—thank you—that's right. No—I'll go right away.'

She saw him turn grey and got a tablet ready to pop under his tongue. Something had happened. To Mitchell! She stopped breathing as she waited for him to speak.

'He's—had an—accident,' James managed faintly. 'Crashed his car. We must go. He's very poorly— they're afraid he—he won't—last the night.'

CHAPTER TEN

AMAZINGLY, Mr Warrender did not suffer another heart attack. It was as though his body somehow knew that he must be strong. Justine drove him to the hospital, organised a wheelchair, and pushed him along silent corridors until they found Mitchell.

She froze when she saw the still, prostrate form. All colour had drained from his face, leaving his tanned skin a sickly yellow. Stripped of his sophisticated veneer he looked vulnerable and innocent, and Justine's heart went out to him.

A nurse sat at his side, keeping a careful eye on the drip that was his life-line. Justine announced who they were, and she smiled and stood up. 'You can have a few minutes alone with him, but he won't know you're here.'

'I understand,' said Justine, glancing worriedly at Mr Warrender, who was staring at his son as though seeing him for the last time.

'I'll fetch Dr Gainswood. He wants to have a word.'

Justine nodded, wheeling her employer close to his son's side where he took a passive hand into his own. Tears spilled down his cheeks, falling in dark round spots on to the bed cover, a sob escaping his throat. 'Don't die, son. Please don't die.'

Justine had never thought to see the day when James Warrender would be the stronger of the two. He gripped Mitchell's hand as though willing life into him, his eyes steady on his son's face.

There was no movement from Mitchell's still figure, not even the merest flicker of an eyelash. If it were not for the monitor which registered his heartbeats, which told them he was breathing, it would have looked as though he were dead.

Justine struggled to hold back her own tears, but there was a lump in her throat threatening to choke her, and her eyes were moist. She silently added her own pleas to his father's.

It was cruel that such a thing should have happened, just when things were going so well between them. And even crueller that it was her fault, even if not intentionally. Again she had caused trauma in the Warrender household.

Becoming involved with them had been madness. She ought to have left when Mitchell first started getting nasty; moved away, emigrated, anything but hang around causing more devastation.

She was jinxed, an inheritance from her mother. They were both bad news for the Warrenders. If Mitchell lived, she would leave and make sure they never set eyes on her again.

If he lived ... Of course he would live! No matter what the doctors said, Mitchell would survive, if only to give her a bad time. He had a reason to live. He would not give up so easily.

But she had to admit he looked at death's door. There were livid cuts and bruises on his face, but no other visible signs of injury. She knew, though, that internal damage was the worst kind.

She glanced at Mr Warrender, but he was oblivious to her presence, his whole attention concentrated on the inert form of his son. He looked positively glowing with health compared with Mitchell's pallor, but Justine knew what this situation could do to him, and kept a vigilant eye on them both.

The nurse returned, and with her Dr Gainswood. He was young, thin and sympathetic. Justine liked him on sight, and as he spoke gently to Mr Warrender, he made it sound as though Mitchell was the most important person in his life, and this was what Mr Warrender needed to hear.

'I have to be honest,' he said at length. 'If he does live, there's a very strong possibility of brain damage.' Justine gasped and glanced at Mr Warrender, touching his arm and gazing speechlessly into his face. This couldn't happen, not to Mitchell. He was so vital, so strong and powerful, so much a man!

Mr Warrender looked grim. 'But you don't know?'

'Not for sure, but it doesn't look good. I wish I had happier news, I really do.' He looked as upset as they felt. 'We can't operate yet, he's too weak. He lost an awful lot of blood, because it was a long time before anyone found him. There was no other vehicle involved. I guess he was going too fast and overshot the bend.'

And all because he had seen her kissing Stewart and interpreted it wrongly! If only he had waited to hear her introduction. If! What a wealth of regret in that one simple word.

She continued to cling to Mr Warrender as the doctor comforted them, wondering how she would live with herself if Mitchell died, or, suffered brain damage. It would be an end to her own life too.

'I suggest you go home now and get some rest,' continued Dr Gainswood. 'We'll ring you if there's any change. He's certainly a lot stronger than he was an hour ago. I didn't hold out much hope for his life then. Now it's a different picture altogether.'

Mr Warrender shook his head, still more tears spilling down his cheeks. 'I can't leave my son.'

'Please,' implored Justine, 'Dr Gainswood's right, you can't do anything. And Mitchell doesn't know you're here. We'll come again in the morning. Let's get some sleep.'

But how would she ever sleep again with this hanging over her head? How would she get any peace?

It was a terrible, terrible thing that had happened, and she felt entirely to blame. If she'd been quicker to say who Stewart was. If she'd gone after him. *If! If! If!* There it was again, that stupid little word.

The doctor handed her a tiny bottle. 'One of these will help Mr Warrender sleep.'

'You're aware that he has a heart condition?' she asked softly.

He nodded. 'He's hanging on well.'

'He's marvellous', smiled Justine. 'They're both as stubborn as mules. Mitchell will pull through, I know he will.' But she wished she felt as confident as she sounded.

Once they were back home she settled Mr Warrender in bed, helped by a worried Mrs Knight, and made him swallow a sleeping pill, sitting by his side until he dropped off before going to bed herself.

But sleep evaded her, and she would not take a tablet in case the hospital rang. Instead she made a jug of coffee and sat in the kitchen drinking cup after cup, her thoughts with Mitchell.

What had he been thinking when he raced out of the house? That she was entertaining another boyfriend whom he knew nothing about? That she was flirting with a guest of his father's? Who knew what conclusion he had drawn?

And now he was lying there, unaware of anyone or anything. His life was suspended. Whether he made it or lost, the outcome rested on his will to live. His subconscious was fighting the battle for him.

Childishly, she crossed her fingers. He must live! But would he want to if he was unable to lead a normal life? If he could not think or speak with the clarity and conciseness that had always been a part of his sharp mind?

She closed her eyes, trying to shut out the horror of such an existence. Mitchell could never accept it. He would rather die than be subject to the degradation of half a life.

She fell asleep in her chair, knowing nothing more until Mrs Knight woke her. It was just getting light. She yawned and stretched, feeling as stiff as a board, wondering for a second why she was here, and then memory returned. 'The hospital, have they phoned?' she asked urgently.

Mrs Knight shook her head.

'Is Mr Warrender awake?'

'No, he'll sleep for a several more hours yet, and I suggest you go to bed as well. How long have you been here?'

'All night,' confessed Justine, and the thought of her soft comfortable bed did appeal. But Mitchell? She must find out about him.

'Tut, tut,' reproved the housekeeper. 'Come on, away with you now.'

Justine nodded. 'I'll ring the hospital first.'

But there was no change. He was still critical although holding his own. And with that she had to be satisfied.

It was mid-morning when they made their next visit. Mitchell still lay with closed eyes, unaware of anything going on around him, but his pulse was stronger.

'If this continues,' confirmed Dr Gainswood, 'we shall soon be doing exploratory surgery.'

'And you'll then be able to tell us whether——' Mr Warrender could not get out the words.

But the doctor understood. He nodded, saying kindly, 'All we can do is pray.'

Justine had already done that, and she was sure Mr Warrender had too. They stayed for several hours, but there was no change in Mitchell's condition and they finally allowed themselves to be sent home.

Gradually, over the next few days, Mitchell's

condition improved. To their relief it looked as though there was no permanent damage done to his brain, although he was still in a coma and the hospital could not be sure. But their visits were no longer so fraught with worry.

Stewart telephoned daily for accounts of Mitchell's progress, and Justine was happy to inform him that things were looking up. 'I think I'd have wanted to kill myself, too, if he'd died,' she said.

He tried telling her that was stupid talk, but he knew how she felt and could sympathise. 'I can't help wondering, though, what will happen when he finally regains consciousness. It might be as well if you keep out of his way for a while.'

Justine agreed, but on the day that Mitchell opened his eyes, she was the first person he saw. And such was her relief that she leaned forward and kissed him, her hot tears wetting his face.

He gazed at her blankly, almost as though he did not recognise her, and then went back to sleep. She looked at Mr Warrender, sitting at the other side of the bed. He was smiling, the first time she had seen him smile in days. 'I think he's going to be all right,' he said, his voice gruff with emotion.

The strain then began to show on the older man. He grew tired and spent more time in bed, and Justine made some visits alone—always, of course, reporting on Mitchell's progress the moment she got back.

He was often asleep, and she spent hours sitting looking at him, The lacerations were healing nicely, the bruises turning a beautiful technicolor, but he had lost that frightening waxen whiteness and the doctor was pleased with his progress.

She longed to touch him, to confess how much she loved him, and did in fact once whisper the words. But his eyelids flickered, and, fearing he had heard, she fled the room.

And then one day, as she sat lost in thought, dreaming that he had completely recovered and accepted her explanation about Stewart, she was startled by a sudden movement.

Mitchell sat bolt upright, staring at her with savage eyes. 'What the hell are you doing here? Where's my father?'

'What I've been doing for the last week,' she whispered, silently pleading with him to understand, 'willing you to get better. Your father's at home. He's all right, but he's very tired. He was here a lot just after your accident.'

'I'd like to see him,' he said, his tone noticeably softening, 'but I don't want you here. I don't want to see you ever again.'

She swallowed a painful lump. 'Why? I thought things were changing between us?' Didn't he love her? Had his father been mistaken when he said Mitchell was jealous? Or hadn't he yet had time to think things over? Was she hoping for too much too soon?

He closed his eyes. 'I don't want to discuss it, Justine. Please go.'

She opened her mouth to try again, then realised she could do more harm than good. When he was fully recovered, when he was home again, perhaps then she would attempt to make him see sense.

But she was reluctant to leave now that he was at last awake and stood by the door for several more seconds, watching him, sending him her love, praying for his in return.

He looked at her, his eyes snapping open as though worked by strings. He said nothing but such was the expression in them that Justine fled, filled with bitter disappointment, almost crying because he wanted nothing more to do with her.

It was what she had half expected, but his father was so sure Mitchell loved her that she had kept on hoping he was right. Now she knew they were the fanciful thoughts of an old man.

But she put on a brave smile when she arrived home. 'Guess what? I've been talking to Mitchell— and he wants to see you.'

Relief such as she had never seen before softened the lines of Mr Warrender's face. His tired grey eyes lightened and he beamed, holding out his arms.

Justine went willingly into them, feeling his cheeks moist against her own. His voice trembled as he asked, 'Take me to him now.'

She drove back the mile or so, but did not go into the ward, instead enlisting the aid of a nurse to push James's wheelchair. 'I'm sure you'd like to be alone,' she whispered, knowing Mr Warrender would never guess her real reason for staying behind.

He was more cheerful that night than she had seen him in a long time. 'There's no danger now; he's going to be all right.' He looked young and carefree, and no one would have guessed he had a weak heart.

'It's a miracle,' breathed Justine, wondering how soon she dared broach the subject of her leaving. She could not be here when Mitchell came home. She refused to be the cause of any more disruption in this household.

'You didn't mention the reason he shot out of the house?' she asked breathlessly, although she was sure he hadn't. There was no evidence that their conversation had been anything other than comfortable.

'No,' James frowned. 'I thought it best to let him bring that up. Did he say anything to you?'

Justine shook her head vaguely and decided there was no point in evading the issue. 'Actually, he didn't seem too pleased to see me.'

Another frown. 'Are you sure?'

'He—he told me he didn't ever want to see me

again.' She had not meant to blurt it out quite so bluntly and held her breath, hoping he would not take it too hard.

He closed his eyes, grimacing. 'He's a fool, but he's also not himself yet. He'll come round, you'll see. Give him another day or two.'

But the next time Justine ventured into Mitchell's ward, she got exactly the same reception. She had left Mr Warrender at home, on his insistence, and driven over alone. Now she wished she had the older man to back her up.

As on the previous occasion, Mitchell was asleep when she got there, or at least his lids were closed, and she pulled up a chair and sat down, greedily feasting her eyes on his handsome face. How much she loved him, and how deeply it hurt that he should reject her.

She wanted to reach out and touch him, to smooth those ugly scars, to kiss them better. She wanted to feel his arms around her, holding her close against his body with renewed strength.

She needed him. She ached with desire. If he banished her, if he still insisted that she walk out of his life, he would be condemning her to a lifetime of regret. Her scars would never heal as his would. She would be permanently damaged.

'Get out!' He spoke without opening his eyes, without giving her any visible sign that he knew she was there.

Justine started and stared. 'We need to talk.'

'What about?'

'Us,' she said faintly.

'There is no us. There is me and there is you. Two entirely separate people. And I don't want you to be a part of my life.' At last he looked at her, his gaze narrowed and disconcerting.

Justine shifted uneasily. 'If you'd only let me explain. It's really very simple. That man was——'

'Justine!' His strong voice effectively silenced her. 'Don't give me your excuses. I was right when I first likened you to your mother. Any man will do so long as he's around when you need him. All I can say is, thank goodness I found out before I made a complete fool of myself—by asking you to marry me.'

Justine gasped, her eyes widening.

'Wouldn't that have been a laugh? I gave you the benefit of the doubt where my father was concerned. I realised I was over-reacting in that direction. But to double-cross me even before I'd got around to asking the question—that is something I cannot stomach.'

He had wanted to marry her? It sounded like a dream come true. She simply had to make him listen to the truth. 'Mitchell, if you'll let me explain, I——'

But again he silenced her. 'I really thought that you felt the same for me as I felt for you. What are you, for heaven's sake—a nymphomaniac?'

He glared at her, and something inside Justine snapped. Whether he was ill or not, he had no right to speak to her like this. She tilted her chin, returning his black look with a belligerent stare of her own.

'If you won't listen to me, and if you don't trust your own judgment, then I agree, there is no point in our seeing one another again. But you're not the winner, Mitchell Warrender. I'm the one who's doing the walking out. I don't want to see you ever again.'

CHAPTER ELEVEN

TEARS raced down Justine's cheeks as she fled from the hospital. She ignored the car and began walking the streets of London, not even noticing when people stopped to stare.

She was not a pretty picture with mascara streaking her cheeks, her eyes wild, hair streaming behind her as she half-ran, half-walked.

She was finished with Mitchell Warrender for all time! He had caused her more heartache in a few months than she had experienced in twenty-four years.

He had accused her of devastating their lives. What did he think *he* had done? He had deliberately set out to ruin her, and yet when he had fallen in love despite himself, he had still somehow managed to turn the tables. She wished with all her heart that she had never met him.

She did not blame Delphine. Her mother could never have envisaged the repercussions her attempted deception would bring. It was Mitchell's own suspicious mind that had done the damage. He had carried his hatred of Delphine for so many years that there was no chance of his ever ridding himself of it. She should have known he would never truly trust her.

With no conscious thought of where she was going, Justine eventually found herself outside Lalage's pretty terraced house. She rang the bell, falling inside when the door opened, conscious of the red-head's curious stare, but more intent on finding refuge than anything else.

A glass of brandy was pushed into her hand, and after a few minutes she was able to speak, appreciating Lalage's respect of her need for silence.

'I'm sorry. I've just lost Mitchell, and I feel awful.'

'Oh, no!' Lalage visibly blanched. 'I thought he was getting better?'

Justine realised what she had said and shook her head, laughing hysterically. 'He's not dead. I've walked out on him. God, he made me so angry. Who does he think he is? A nymphomaniac, indeed! I can count on one hand the number of boyfriends I've had. He's the one who's warped. He's got an evil mind— and I'm better off without him.' And then she broke down and cried all over again.

Lalage let her get on with it, digesting the information Justine had thrown at her, drawing her own conclusions but saying nothing.

'Do you think I'm a fool?' asked Justine at length, twisting her sopping handkerchief between her fingers.

'Not at all. You're overwrought. You've not had an easy time lately. Did he really call you that?'

She looked amused, and this made Justine even angrier. 'He did! If he hadn't been lying in his silly hospital bed, I'd have kicked him where it hurt.'

'Had his accusations anything to do with Stewart?'

'Everything,' acknowledged Justine. 'He thinks he's some boyfriend I've kept hidden. He wouldn't even let me explain.' Her voice rose, and she laughed. 'First he thought I was after an affair with his father, now my own brother. He's sick. He's demented. He wants certifying!'

Lalage laid a hand in her arm. 'Calm yourself, Justine, you're being irrational.'

'Irrational?' she screamed. 'You haven't heard Mitchell. Goodness me, he takes some beating. I——'

'Justine!' interrupted Lalage worriedly. 'Forget

him. Don't go on like this. If he bothers you that much, he's not worth wasting your breath on.'

'I know,' Justine declared loudly, 'but I can't sit down under insults like that. It's all he's ever done since we met—insult me. I wish I was a man. He wouldn't get away with it then.'

'It's as well you're not,' said Lalage. 'They send you to prison for murder, and it looks as though that's what you have in mind.'

Justine did indeed feel murderous, and her eyes flashed. 'It would be a lot better than having to put up with what he doles out.' She clenched her fists and pounded them fiercely on the arm of her chair, her voice shrill. 'If he ever tries to——'

When Lalage's hand struck her cheek, she stopped, looked resentful, and then dropped her head into her hands, all the fight draining out of her.

'I'm sorry I had to do that.' Lalage really did look apologetic. 'But you were getting hysterical. He's not worth it, Justine. No man is. You're better off without him.'

Justine nodded. 'I shall have to leave, of course, before he comes out of hospital. Goodness knows what his father will say, but it can't be helped. I can't go through anything like this again.'

'Where will you go?' asked Lalage anxiously.

'I think I might go abroad, start afresh,' said Justine thoughtfully. 'I was at college with a girl who's now designing in Italy. I think I might go there. With my experience it should be relatively easy to find a job— unless Mitchell puts his spoke in the wheel there, too.'

'Don't tell him,' said Lalage. 'But you can't go before the wedding. We want you to be bridesmaid.'

Justine's eyes widened. 'You've fixed the date?'

Lalage smiled and nodded.

'Why didn't you tell me?'

'We only decided a couple of days ago. The house is

going through quicker than we expected, so we saw no point in hanging on.'

'I don't blame you,' said Justine, wondering why she hadn't noticed that Lalage was glowing with happiness. She had been so full of her own troubles that she hadn't bothered to look at her brother's fiancée properly.

She and Stewart were so much in love it was impossible not to feel faintly envious. If only things had been different between her and Mitchell! If! There it was again, the annoying little word that meant so much!

'We're getting married three weeks on Saturday. Think you can hold out that long? You're welcome to stay here.'

Justine grimaced and nodded. It would upset Stewart if she missed his wedding. Besides, there was no chance of meeting Mitchell again. Their affair, if you could call it that, was over. Things had been said that could never be retracted. So far as she was concerned, he no longer existed, and he probably felt the same way.

'Good. We'll go now and pick up your things. You might as well make the break while you're in the mood. We don't want Mr Warrender persuading you to change your mind.'

Justine sighed. 'He's the one person I shall miss— and he won't like it. He's always saying what a difference I've made to his life.'

'That's why I'm coming with you,' said Lalage firmly. 'I know how easily you allow yourself to be swayed.'

'Not this time,' assured Justine. 'I've reached my limit.'

They collected the car from the hospital, and as she had expected, Mr Warrender was very upset. 'Justine, my dear, Mitchell's not himself. You mustn't believe everything he says,' he pleaded.

They were sitting on the terrace overlooking the park, a tray of tea and a plate of scones in front of them. Justine had not told Mr Warrender exactly what had gone on between her and Mitchell, just that he was being extremely disagreeable and she could not possibly live in Regent's Park any longer.

'He meant what he said, all right,' declared Justine, blue eyes flashing, 'and I meant what I said to him—that I never want to see him again.'

'Please——' implored the older man, 'please, Justine, give yourself time to calm down. Decisions made in haste are rarely the right ones.'

Justine watched a blackbird devouring a worm, pulling it out of the lawn and swallowing it mercilessly. That was what would happen to her if she stayed here. Mitchell would devour her. He had already gone a long way towards making her life a misery. Why commit herself to a living hell?

She shook her head. 'Mitchell and I are incompatible. We'll never see eye to eye. It was a mistake coming here. I'm sorry, Mr Warrender, I really am.'

He looked sad and old and beaten. 'Mitchell's not here all the time. Couldn't we work something out?' It was a last attempt to persuade her to change her mind.

'I don't think so,' she said. 'There'd be no telling when he might turn up. I'd be a nervous wreck.'

He closed his eyes and Justine looked worriedly across at Lalage, who had remained silent while they were talking.

'He'll be all right,' mouthed the red-head.

Justine hoped so, she really did. It would be the last straw if anything happened to Mitchell's father now.

'Where are you going to live?' he enquired suddenly, his eyes pinning her. 'What are you going to do for money?'

'I'm going abroad,' said Justine swiftly, with a defiant look at Lalage.

'That means I won't see you again,' frowned James Warrender.

Justine determinedly hardened her heart. 'I'm afraid so. I'll write, and I'll visit you if ever I come back for a holiday.' But she would never give him her address. There was no way she wanted Mitchell finding out where she was.

Their final goodbye was heart-breaking. Justine cried and Mr Warrender's eyes were moist. 'If things don't work out, there's always a home for you here,' he said. 'Don't forget that, Justine.'

'I won't,' she sobbed. 'I do love you, and I hate myself for what I'm doing to you, but——'

'You have your own life to lead,' he sighed. 'I know, my dear. I understand. It was foolish of me to think you'd be happy here after the way Mitchell treated you. I guess all I've done is push you even further apart.'

'No!' cried Justine. 'Don't ever think that. I don't blame you for hoping that Mitchell would fall in love with me. I hoped it myself. But fate has decreed otherwise.'

'Do you still love him?'

'I don't know,' she admitted huskily. 'I don't know what I feel any more. At this very moment I hate him, but that will pass, and then——who knows? That's why I have to go away, right away. I can't risk ever seeing him again.'

'Poor Justine,' he whispered. 'And poor Delphine. She was never happy either. I wish I knew the answer. I'd willingly give away every penny I possess to see you and Mitchell make a go of it.'

'I think we should go,' said Lalage softly.

Justine nodded, glad of the interruption. Goodbyes were always sad occasions, and this one particularly so.

'Goodbye, Mr Warrender,' she sobbed.

'Goodbye, my sweet little girl. Think of me sometimes.'

'Always,' she said. 'Always.'

During the next three weeks, Lalage deliberately kept Justine busy. There was so much to do: packing; shopping for furniture and carpets for the new house; buying the wedding dress and trousseau; writing out lists; sending out invitations.

Justine made her own plans. She wrote to Debra in Italy and received an immediate reply offering a share of her apartment.

'You're in luck,' Debra wrote. 'My flat-mate's just moved out and I was looking for someone else, and my boss has been talking for ages about finding another designer. I've told him about you, so you're in with a chance.'

She went on to say how great it would be to see Justine again, how much she missed her English friends, though the Italian boys made up for it! There was no one special yet, but she was keeping her fingers crossed.

Obviously, thought Justine, there was someone she had her eye on ... she felt a faint misgiving. To see another romance blossom, when there was no hope for herself, would be pretty devastating.

The day of the wedding dawned to clear blue skies and the sun shining for the lovers. Lalage looked particularly beautiful in a genuine antique lace dress that she had found by accident in a back-street second-hand shop.

Justine wore pale aquamarine, with silk flowers dyed to match in her hair. Stewart looked handsome in his morning dress, and even Gerald seemed kindly disposed that day.

There must have been at least a hundred guests, and the reception was in a marquee in the grounds of Holt House. How proud Delphine would have been!

Lalage and Stewart were going to Scotland for a few days' honeymoon, and then straight in to their new home. The furniture was being removed from the terraced house on Monday and Justine was flying to Italy the same evening. It was all arranged down to the last detail.

Sunday she spent completely alone. She thought about phoning Mr Warrender, but did not want him to know that she had not yet left the country. The hospital confirmed, when she rang them, that Mitchell had been discharged, so she knew the old man would not be alone.

That night she slept little. It was all very well telling herself she did not want to see Mitchell again, but she could not ignore the persistent ache in her heart. She loved him still. She guessed she always would.

The removal van came and emptied the house. The weather had changed and it was raining. It suited her mood. All that was left was herself and three cases. Not much for almost a quarter of a century's living. But she was off to a new start and there was no point in being morbid. She would order the taxi now and spend the next few hours in the airport rather than in this empty house.

But the phone rang before she could pick it up. It was probably Stewart wanting to wish her all the best. She smiled. How nice of him to think of her, even on honeymoon.

'Justine, I want to talk to you.'

This wasn't Stewart. Only Mitchell's voice could send that tingle down her spine. She curled up inside as she answered. 'I'm sorry, didn't I make myself clear? I don't want to speak to you.' And she slammed down the receiver.

For a minute she could not move. She felt as if she

had been turned to stone. What did he want? How had he known she was here? His father should have told him she'd left the country. And she was wasting time!

Suddenly galvanised into action, she lifted the receiver again and dialled a taxi, waiting in a dither for it to arrive. Then, through the window, she saw Mitchell's car slide to a halt outside.

'Oh no,' she groaned, and wondered whether she dared pretend there was no one in. But one half of her still wanted to see him, no matter what the other said, and she opened the door to his ring.

He wasted no time, pushing past her. Then he saw the empty rooms and her waiting cases. 'Just in time, I see.'

For what? she wondered, but said nothing, staring at him hungrily. She would never see him again. She wanted to imprint every tiny detail in her memory.

His black, tight-fitting trousers and black cashmere sweater made him seem sinister on this miserable day. He still wore the scars of his accident and had lost weight. His chiselled cheekbones were prominent, his eyes sunken, his tan faded. He did not look at all well.

'Should you be here?' she asked sharply. 'You look as though you ought still to be in bed.'

'How would I see you otherwise?' he demanded, his eyes fixed fiercely on hers.

'Would it have mattered if you didn't?' she asked tiredly, banishing the fleeting thought that he might have had a change of heart. His set face told its own story.

'To me, yes,' he said quietly. 'How about you?'

Justine hardened her heart. 'I'd rather not have this meeting. I can see no point in it.'

'Why didn't you tell me he was your brother?' His tone was accusing.

'Stewart?' The unexpected question made Justine blink owlishly. 'You didn't give me a chance.'

'You didn't try very hard.'

'Because it was like banging my head against a brick wall,' she replied smartly. 'Besides, I don't think much of a man who condemns without a hearing.'

He looked guilty. 'So I've spoiled whatever chance I might have had with you?'

'That's right,' said Justine quickly. 'And I don't know how you knew I was here, but I wish you'd go.'

'Father said you'd left the country,' he accused. 'If it hadn't been for this——' He took a newspaper cutting from his breast pocket and thrust it at her '—I might never have found you.'

Justine unfolded the slip of paper and saw Lalage and Stewart, herself and Gerald, smiling happily as all bridal groups do. There had been many photographers at the wedding and she had not realised any were from the press. She should have done. Gerald was still a well-known man in the City.

'So?' she said. 'I'm going now. My taxi will be here any moment, and then you'll never see me again. I'm sorry if I'm spoiling your sport. It must have been fun, seeing how far you could push me.'

'Justine, don't!' he groaned. 'This is hard enough without your making it worse.'

She jutted her chin. 'What's hard?'

'Telling you that I've been a fool. That I ought to be horsewhipped.' His voice dropped to a mere whisper and she noticed how grey he was about the mouth. 'That I love you.'

He watched her closely as he made his revelation, seeing the sudden widening of her beautiful blue eyes, the wariness, the fear.

'This is not another plot to bring you down.' His eyes implored her. 'I shall never hurt you again as long as I live. I've been acting like a spiteful child. Can you ever forgive me?'

Justine was afraid to speak. Had his father told him

that she loved him? Had he spurred Mitchell into making this confession? James Warrender had always felt that Mitchell loved her, and it looked now as though he was right. There was pain in his eyes; deep down pain that had to be sincere.

But she was still reluctant to accept his word. How did she know she could trust him? His lack of faith, his obsession that she had to be a carbon copy of Delphine just because they looked alike, how did she know these suspicions would not raise their ugly heads again? He was asking too much.

'Justine! I'm waiting.'

She took a deep breath and stood firm. 'I'm sorry, Mitchell. I can't.'

'But why? What do I have to do, get down on my knees and grovel?' His face was distinctly ashen now. 'I'll do that if I have to. I love you, Justine. I want to marry you. And I know you love me.'

So his father had told him. Damn! How could she fight her way out of this? Because fight she had to. There was no way she was going to admit her feelings and commit herself to an unhappy marriage.

Mitchell had a deranged mind, something that no amount of surgery would cure. He might be genuinely sorry now, but later who knew what he might feel? His father's dogged ill-health, for one thing, would be a perpetual reminder.

'It was a long time ago when I told your father. A lot has happened since then.'

'My father? He knows how you feel?' Mitchell looked shocked.

Justine frowned. 'It wasn't he who told you?'

'Certainly not. You told me yourself.'

By her actions? By her spontaneous responses to his lovemaking? Why hadn't she been more careful?

'You don't remember?'

'I don't recall telling you in so many words,' she

said distantly, trying to look aloof but afraid she was
failing. Of its own accord, her heart began to pound,
her body to respond. She did love him. Yes, she did.
But she must never admit it, never give in to her
heart's desire. It would be madness.

He smiled, the harsh contours of his face softening.
'Perhaps you didn't intend me to hear, but it was your
words that made me better, Justine. They made me
fight for my life. I did a lot of thinking in my hospital
bed. I came to my senses. And when you said you
loved me, I knew everything was going to be all right.'

As he spoke, Justine recalled her softly spoken
words. She had forgotten them until this moment.
And she had never dreamt that he had heard.

She shrugged. 'You had a strange way of showing
it.'

He hung his head. 'I found it difficult to forget what
I thought you'd done.'

'And now? Do you really think you'll ever forget
now? Won't it happen all over again if you see me
speaking to another man?'

'I'll never forget how foolish I've been,' he said
quietly. 'I don't think either of us will forget that. But
I would like to think that you could find it in your
heart to forgive me. I know it's a lot to ask, but——'

'You're right, it is a lot,' cried Justine. 'Go away,
Mitchell. I can't take the risk of your hurting me
again.'

'Justine!' He came towards her, arms outstretched.
'I'll never hurt you again, not so long as I live. I
promise.'

She backed. Once he touched her, it would be all
over. The space separating them was her only
salvation.

'You can't bear me to touch you now?' Pain ravaged his
face, twisting and tormenting, turning his eyes into
deep pits of despair. 'It's what I deserve, I suppose.'

He was silent for a moment. 'Is there any hope? Or must I let you go wherever it is I've driven you to?'

'I want to go,' whispered Justine, against her real wishes. But it was for the best.

'Where are you going?'

'Italy,' she admitted.

'You have somewhere to live?'

She nodded.

'And a job?'

'I hope so.'

He looked grim. 'Warrender's have a branch there, as you probably know. If you're stuck, get in touch with them. Mention my name. I'll see you get fixed up.'

Justine supposed there was a funny side to the situation somewhere, but for the life of her she couldn't see it. Did he think he was so big, offering to help now when it was his fault she'd been out of work in the first place?

'No thanks,' she said tightly. 'Whatever I do will be by my own efforts.'

The taxi honked outside. 'So this really is the end?' he asked tonelessly.

She nodded.

'Would you permit me to drive you to the airport?'

Although Justine knew she ought to put an end to it all now, she could not resist the thought of spending more time with him. She nodded, even while she told herself it was a wrong decision.

He smiled briefly and went outside to dismiss the taxi. When he came back, she had composed herself. She would treat him coolly; show him that she had no intention of ever changing her mind.

But she had forgotten what it was like sitting side by side with him in his car. The intimacy, his special male odour, his nearness, the throbbing of her heart!

Her mouth felt dry and she swallowed, trying to

concentrate on the hypnotic rhythm of the windscreen wipers, seeing nothing outside, conscious only of Mitchell.

He was silent, outwardly concentrating on the busy London traffic made more hazardous by the driving rain. But she guessed that inside he was equally tormented.

It had taken his accident to make him realise that he loved her. Even now she could not really accept that he was sincere. He desired her, she knew that, the physical attraction had always been there, but did his feelings go deep enough for a lifetime's commitment? Could he ever forget she was Delphine's daughter?

The fact that she could not give a positive yes to these questions told her she was doing the right thing in rejecting him. It was hard, it was the hardest thing she had ever done, but she would get over him—in time. How long was debatable, but time healed everything, or so she'd heard.

They were on the motorway nearing Heathrow before he spoke. 'I've always loved you, Justine, do you know that? Right from the day you walked into my office. But because you looked so like Delphine, I forced myself to hate you. I now accept that your mother wasn't as promiscuous and cold-blooded as I thought—and I no longer blame her for her conduct to my father.'

Justine listened, her heart beating even faster, almost drowning out his words. If this were true, it put a whole new complexion on things. She felt him glance at her, but deliberately kept her face expressionless, almost as if she hadn't heard.

'I mean it, Justine. I can stifle my feelings no longer. Tell me it's not too late—please.' It was a cry from the heart.

She let out a long shuddering breath, her hands clenched tightly together on her lap, and made one last valiant effort to preserve her future happiness. 'No, I can't.' Her voice was faint, almost inaudible, but Mitchell heard and his knuckles gleamed white on the wheel.

He put his foot down on the accelerator and shot past the turning they should have taken for the airport.

'Mitchell, what are you doing?' she cried, but he did not answer, his face grim, his speed going up and up until Justine feared for their safety.

At the next junction he left the motorway and finally slewed on to a patch of waste ground. He switched off the engine and braked, then turned, took one hard, hungry look at her, and pulled her into his arms.

'I didn't want to use emotional blackmail,' he said hoarsely, 'but it seems there's no other way.' And before she could protest, his mouth claimed hers.

From that moment, Justine knew she was lost. She drank in his kisses eagerly, not even putting up a fight. Perhaps they had both known from the very beginning what the outcome of their relationship would be. They had choosen to ignore it, carving instead a path of destruction which could so easily have broken both their hearts.

By the time he released her, her whole body throbbed and she knew irrevocably that she would never let him go.

'Tell me again it's too late,' he grated, his eyes crazed with desire, a pulse beating rapidly in his temple, his jaw clenched. He looked as though he was going out of his mind, and Justine felt sorry for him.

'I love you,' she whispered huskily. 'I can't deny it any longer.'

'You've forgiven me?'

She nodded, closing her eyes, feeling his arms tighten around her and accepting once again his hungry mouth. This time there was tenderness, caring, respect.

'I'll make it up to you, my love, I promise,' he murmured, showering her face with kisses, looking deeply into her eyes, questioning her still.

'Let's just forget the whole thing,' said Justine. 'It was a nightmare while it lasted, but now it's over. Let's not mention it again.'

'I don't deserve you,' he groaned. 'I pulled everything from under your feet, and kicked you while you were down. I hate myself.'

'Don't. Please, don't,' she whispered, touching his face, tracing each jutting bone, his sculpted sensual lips, the thick lashes around his tormented eyes.

They clung desperately, drawing strength from one another. Time lost all meaning, but gradually they grew calmer.

He sat back in his seat and smiled. 'Tell me I'm dreaming, my beautiful friend. Tell me it's not true you actually love me.'

Justine's smile was wide, her face radiant. 'Mitchell, I love you. I want to marry you. I want to spend the rest of my life with you. And I think we should go home and tell your father.'

'How naturally you say home. I like that. And I'm glad you like my father—he loves you dearly. He'll be so happy.'

'Did you know'—an impish smile dimpled Justine's cheeks—'that he once tried to bribe me into marrying you?'

His eyes widened. 'The old rogue. When was that?'

'When he was in hospital. A sort of last wish to make an old man happy. He knew you loved me. He's very astute. Naturally I didn't believe him and would hear none of it.'

Mitchell shook his head. 'I wonder how he was going to pull that off? Was that when you told him you loved me?'

She nodded.

'He never said a word,' Mitchell chuckled. 'He's let us get on with making a mess of our lives. I suppose now he's going to say "I told you so".'

'I imagine he will,' smiled Justine, 'and he'll thoroughly enjoy it.'

'No more than I shall enjoy telling him about us.' He gave her one last lingering kiss before turning the key and setting the car into motion.

Justine leaned back in her seat, smiling happily, imagining James Warrender's face when he heard the news, but more than anything trying to imagine herself married to Mitchell. Who would have thought that this black day would turn out so perfectly? The rain still poured, the sky was thunderous, but so far as she was concerned the sun was shining. She was happier than she had ever been in her life.

She looked at Mitchell, touched his arm, feeling suddenly shy. 'Thank you for loving me.'

'No!' He shook his head violently. 'I'm the one who should do the thanking. I thank you for understanding me, for being so generous, for loving me despite all I've done. You're one in a million, Justine. I know I've put you through hell, and I'm deeply sorry.'

'I thought we weren't going to mention that again?' she reproved gently.

'It's such a terrible thing I did, how can I forget?' he groaned.

'If I can, why not you?'

He smiled and nodded slowly. 'There's only one thing that will take my mind off the past.'

'And that is?' she prompted.

'Making arrangements for our wedding.'

She grinned. 'You're on. The moment we get back—after telling your father, of course—we'll fix a date.'

'Like tomorrow?' he suggested eagerly.

'How impatient can you get?' she scoffed. 'I thought at least the day after.' Then, on a more serious note, 'I know you don't like living in London very much, Mitchell, but would you object strongly to making our home with your father? The house is big enough, and—well, he won't be here forever, and I do love him so.'

'Even London looks different now I know you love me,' he said. 'I don't mind at all. In fact, I wanted to suggest it myself, but I thought all new brides liked a home of their own.'

'It will be ours one day,' she said, 'and until then I'm quite content to share with your father.'

'So long as you don't spend too much time with him,' he threatened. 'You'll be my property, remember? You might look like your mother, but he has no claim on you at all.'

'Except as the daughter he always wanted.'

He nodded. 'The Warrender family will be doing a lot of celebrating tonight. And I bet the old devil's already got a bottle of champagne on ice.'

Justine nodded. 'I wouldn't be at all surprised.'

Harlequin Presents

Coming Next Month

Available in April wherever paperback books are sold, or through Harlequin Reader Service:

In the U.S.
P.O. Box 1397
Buffalo, N.Y.
14240-1397

In Canada
P.O. Box 603
Fort Erie, Ontario
L2A 5X3

Can you keep a secret?

You can keep this one plus 4 free novels

For the millions who can't read
Give the Gift of Literacy

One out of five adults in North America
cannot read or write well enough
to fill out a job application
or understand the directions on a bottle of medicine.

**You can change all this by joining the fight
against illiteracy.**

For more information write to:
Contact, Box 81826, Lincoln, Neb. 68501
In the United States, call toll free: 800-228-3225

**The only degree you need
is a degree of caring**

"This ad made possible with the cooperation of the Coalition for Literacy and the Ad Council."
Give the Gift of Literacy Campaign is a project of the book and periodical industry,
in partnership with Telephone Pioneers of America.